IN GEORGIA
A YANKEE FAMILY IN
THE SEGREGATED SOUTH

BOOKS BY JEROME GOLD

FICTION

In Georgia: A Yankee Family in the Segregated South
The Moral Life of Soldiers
Sergeant Dickinson (originally titled *The Negligence of Death*)
The Prisoner's Son
The Inquisitor
Of Great Spaces (with Les Galloway)

POETRY
Stillness
Prisoners

NONFICTION
In the Spider's Web: a Nonfiction Novel
The Burg and Other Seattle Scenes (Mostly True Stories)
The Divers and Other Mysteries of Seattle (and California, but Just a
    Little): More Mostly True Stories
Paranoia & Heartbreak: Fifteen Years in a Juvenile Facility
How I Learned That I Could Push the Button
Obscure in the Shade of the Giants: Publishing Lives, Volume II
Publishing Lives Volume I: Interviews with Independent
    Book Publishers
Hurricanes (editor)

IN GEORGIA
A YANKEE FAMILY IN
THE SEGREGATED SOUTH

Jerome Gold

Black Heron Press
Post Office Box 13396
Mill Creek, Washington 98082
www.blackheronpress.com

Several of the stories in this book were originally published in whole
or in part in *Moon City Review* or in the following collections: *The
Moral Life of Soldiers*, *The Divers*, *The Burg*, *Prisoners*, and *Of Great
Spaces*. "On the Bus," and "Tragedy in the Desert" are published here
for the first time.

Cover photograph: Whitehall Street, Atlanta, Georgia 1864, courtesy
of the National Archives.

ISBN (print): 978-1-936364-27-5
ISBN (ebook): 978-1-936364-28-2

Black Heron Press
Post Office Box 13396
Mill Creek, Washington 98082
www.blackheronpress.com

For Jeanne

CONTENTS

IN GEORGIA—A YANKEE FAMILY IN THE SEGREGATED SOUTH

I. Paul's Father at the Beginning of the War

On the morning Japan bombed Pearl Harbor, Paul's father was racing Adolphe Menjou, the actor, across the Arizona desert to California. Adolphe Menjou was driving a yellow roadster, Paul's father a forest green convertible. Both men were having the time of their lives.

Six months later, driving east across Texas, Paul's father was chased by a tornado following Route 66. Outside a town a Mexican woman with thirteen kids, or maybe twelve, ran out onto the highway, forcing Paul's father to veer wildly to avoid driving into her or her children. Paul's father did not stop. The tornado blackened the town on either side of the road behind him and then it took the woman and her children.

When Paul's father told the story of the woman and her children—when Paul was thirteen or fourteen and beginning to pull away from his father—he did not emphasize but left implicit their differentness from him, from him and Paul. And anyway, if he had stopped, he could not have saved her and her children, not all of them. And who would decide who would not fit in the car? Anyway, there was no time, not even to stop for one—one child, or the woman alone, perhaps. What did Paul expect from him? Should he have died with them to show solidarity?

Many years after the episode in Texas, driving east again, but through New Mexico, Paul's father was once more pursued by a tornado. In the car with him were Paul's mother, his sister, and Paul. This time, the tornado gaining on them but still a mile or two behind, he stopped and turned the car and drove back west into the twister as fast as he could get the car to go. It was a 1946 Lincoln Cosmopolitan and it weighed more than two tons. It had a V12 engine and it went unswervingly, if with some hesitation, directly into and through the storm. Afterward sand was pitted into the fenders of the car an eighth of an inch and you could hardly see through the windshield.

When Paul's father told this story to Paul's uncles and their wives, he did not say that other cars with smaller engines had not turned, but had outrun the twister. Paul and his family met some of their passengers at a café when Paul's father's windshield was being replaced. Paul's father risked the lives of his wife, his daughter, his son, himself. For what?

When he was older, Paul understood that his father had loved speed, hated moral quandaries. And, given the chance to survive, he had loved the violence of embracing his enemy whom he loved more than Paul's mother, his sister, Paul. Though, to be accurate, when he and Adolphe

Menjou heard on their respective radios the news about Pearl Harbor, both men slowed their cars.

II. Paul's Father and Paul's Uncle Bernie

When Paul was a boy, he used to go out to the desert with his father and his uncle Bernie, ostensibly to shoot rabbits. Once they followed a mountain lion's tracks until Bernie said, "What are we going to do if we find it?" They were carrying .22-caliber rifles and, from its tracks, they knew it was a big cat.

Once Paul shot a bird at what he thought was a far distance. It turned out to be a hummingbird. Suddenly, seeing it so small and dead, knowing that he had done it, his heart felt as though it were breaking apart. His father said, "Don't you feel bad?" Paul could not say anything. He thought he would cry if he tried to speak.

The best parts about being out with Bernie and his father were driving east through the San Bernadino mountains in the morning, into the sun and what they knew would be a scorching day, and listening to the car radio— the Bob and Ray Show, which made Paul laugh—and then later, after they had walked for a couple of hours, building a small fire so they could have coffee or, in Paul's case, chocolate, and telling stories of their lives. Paul did not tell stories, of course, because he hadn't lived long yet and both his father and Bernie had passed through what Paul was experiencing in his life. Also, Paul did not wish to confide the private parts of his life to them.

Bernie would talk to Paul's father about Elaine, his wife, whom he continued to find desirable, and his son who could piss a stream five or six feet long. When Paul looked at him in disbelief, Bernie said, "Little boys can do that. You lose it as you get older, even at your age." Paul was twelve.

Bernie would talk, too, about his experiences in the navy. He had been in the Battle of the Coral Sea in World War II. He told Paul once that when he was in Hong Kong after the war, another sailor, a larger man, had threatened him. Paul did not know if he had threatened to kill Bernie or to beat him up, but Bernie had been scared. But then he had gotten tired of being scared and had fought the man, using a chair leg to beat him until he could not get up. Afterward, the man left him alone; he was afraid of Bernie now.

Paul's father had not been in the war, at least not as a combatant. He had been on the Manhattan Project at the University of Chicago. Since adolescence, he had been responsible for supporting his mother and sister; his mother did not speak English and his sister spent most of her life in mental institutions. He had had scholarship offers from several universities, including MIT and Stanford, but had had to turn them down in order to work. He went to night school for several years, but never earned a degree.

During the war, the navy had offered to commission him and send him to college to study electrical engineering, but the government would not release him. So he missed out not only on a first-rate education, but also on that indefinable thing that binds men to one another after they have suffered hardship together.

Out in the desert, Paul's father told a story about something that happened after the war. He had been working at Argonne National Laboratories on the edge of the Argonne Forest outside of Chicago. One of the things his particular laboratory did was to separate usable uranium from its ore. Part of the process they employed involved baking the ore in a lead-lined oven.

One day Senator Joseph McCarthy came to inspect the laboratory. Senator McCarthy's star was rising then and he was looking for treasonous persons and acts of perfidy by which to boost it further. During his inspection, Senator McCarthy noted that the uranium ore weighed less when it came out of the baking oven than it did when it was placed inside. The laboratory manager explained that the loss of weight was owing to a chemical reaction between the ore and the lining of the oven.

Senator McCarthy was not to be deceived. He wondered aloud who in the laboratory might be selling the missing uranium to the Russians. He said he would return to re-inspect.

When Senator McCarthy returned, he noted that the uranium ore weighed more coming out of the oven than when it was placed inside. The engineers knew that this was due to the chemical reaction between the ore and the new brick lining of the oven. But they said nothing and waited for the senator's reaction. Their anxiety was needless, for Senator McCarthy was content.

Around this time, someone in Paul's father's laboratory began to wonder what was being done with the radioactive waste the laboratory was producing. Someone asked the engineers and finally one of them admitted that he had been filling Mason jars with it, then burying the jars in the forest. He had not mapped the places where he had buried the jars.

When Paul's father finished telling this story, Bernie laughed about Senator McCarthy and said how typically governmental Senator McCarthy's last response was and how it reminded him of the navy. Then he asked how dangerous was the radioactive waste in the Mason jars.

Paul's father shrugged. He said that not only didn't anyone know where they were buried, but nobody knew how many there were; the man who had buried them hadn't counted them.

III. Paul's Father and the Sailor

Once, a friend of Paul's mother brought her new boyfriend to Paul's parents' house. This was during the war in Korea, when Paul's family lived in Georgia. The boyfriend was in a swabbie's uniform and he made a remark about men who had not served in the military in the last war, even though he himself was obviously too young to have been in. Paul's father smiled and put out his hand as though to shake the younger man's. The sailor extended his own hand and suddenly he was upside down against the far wall of the living room and then he fell off it onto the sofa and rolled off the sofa onto the floor.

"Oh, Herb," Paul's mother said.

Paul's father was smiling genuinely now and offered his

hand again, this time to help the other man up. The other man raised his hand, then withdrew it.

"It's all right," Paul's father said. "I made my point."

The sailor put out his hand and Paul's father helped him to his feet. Facing each other, each smiled, Paul's father in friendship, the sailor as though not knowing what to think. The two women laughed from nervous relief. Paul and his sister stared in awe at their father.

They had never seen him do anything like this before. He was not an especially physical man, as they knew him. He did not go in for violent sports, he did not hunt or fish as some of his friends did. Four years later, when he and Bernie and Paul went out into the desert after rabbits, Paul's father did not shoot; he did not even carry a rifle.

So the sailor got to his feet and he and Paul's father stared at each other, each wearing a kind of smile, and the women laughed and then there was talk and movement and noise as everybody went into the dining room for supper.

IV. What Paul's Parents Did in Georgia (I)

Paul's parents had grown up in Chicago and Paul and his sister were born there, but they all moved to Georgia because his sister was ill and her doctors said she would not live to be ten unless their parents took her to live in a warmer climate. Paul's father found work at the Lockheed plant in Marietta.

After two or three years, Paul's father decided that

he wanted to be his own boss and he and Paul's mother thought they could make a success of a restaurant. They opened it in a new shopping center. Its patrons, at least at first, were the workmen who were still building the shops and stores that would compose the center.

Restaurant work was harder than Paul's parents had anticipated, and unrelenting. Paul's father took a leave of absence from Lockheed. Paul's mother worked a regular shift as a cook and also supervised the staff when Paul's father was busy elsewhere. Paul bussed and washed dishes. He worked nine hours a day in the summer and on weekends and holiday breaks from school, and his parents worked longer. His father, a small man, lost forty pounds in his first six months as a restaurant owner.

One evening after closing, seven or eight months after the restaurant opened, Paul sat with his mother, his father, and one of the waitresses at a table. They were taking a break from cleaning up. It was the night they buffed and waxed the floor and Paul had been operating the buffer. The adults were talking about inconsequential things and Paul was listening. Finally somebody decided that they needed to get back to work and they all stood up. Except Paul's mother. She could not get up. Her body would not obey her. She started crying, and either Paul's father or the waitress sent Paul on an errand to the kitchen. But Paul did not go. He stayed and watched, and in a moment the weakness passed and his mother stopped crying and pushed away from the table and stood up.

Paul's mother got away from cooking by hiring a man named Curtis Baron. He was a good cook and Paul's parents appreciated his ability. In turn, Curtis appreciated their giving him a job because he was not long out of the state prison in Alabama and not everybody was willing to hire an ex-convict. Curtis was personable as well as a good cook, and he was careful not to offend anyone.

Eventually, after he became comfortable with Paul's parents, he boasted to them that he had more of their silverware at home than they had in their restaurant. They told him to bring it in and he did, in an old army duffel bag. He was right: he had more than Paul's parents had.

They fired him and Paul's mother took over the cooking responsibilities again. But they let him hang around the restaurant because they still liked him and he had no other place to go to be with people. Occasionally Paul's parents hired him to fill a shift when Paul's mother was too tired or had something else to do. Each day after he worked a shift, Paul's mother or father would ask Curtis to return the silverware he had taken the day before. (He seemed to steal only when he was working, as though he saw it as part of his job.) Usually he did, but sometimes he did not, swearing on the latter occasions that he had not stolen any this time, he did not know why.

Finally he left. He told Paul that he was going to leave, that he thought the police were after him, that they believed he had done some burglaries, and the next day he did not come in to the restaurant.

After a few days Paul's parents began to wonder where Curtis was, they had not seen him in a while, and a few days later Paul told them that Curtis had said he was going to go down to Florida. Paul had waited to tell them because he did not know what they might already know, nor what they might do with their knowledge, and he wanted Curtis to get away. Paul's father counted the silverware but could not tell if any was missing.

V. The Last Best Day

They have just come out of the movie house and now Paul's parents and his sister have gone into the supermarket, leaving him to stand at the far edge of the parking lot overlooking the remains of a mixed forest—loblolly pines and hickories and cow oaks—and then, farther, the four-lane highway, and beyond that a lowland swamp.

He is standing at the verge of a shopping center newly built on a high hill they have sliced the top off of to make a level place for commerce and traffic. The sky is pale blue and small white clouds drift across it and he is ten years old and he is wearing a blue and green checked windbreaker, his favorite jacket, against the chill fall day and he has just come out of a movie and he is standing on what is the top of the remains of a hill beside the family car and he's nearly on a level with the small clouds, looking down past the trees onto the plain and the swamp beyond, and he knows exactly where he is and where he belongs and he is ten and he is wearing his favorite jacket and it is the last best day in the history of the world.

VI. The First Dead Man Paul Ever Saw

Paul saw his first dead man one day when he was walking home from school. It was late winter, the beginning of spring. Leaves were green, but sparse. The road he followed took him along the flank of a hill.

At the bottom, the dead man lay. Two men were walking away from him, starting up toward the road. Paul was certain the man was dead, though he could not have said how he knew. Maybe because the man looked so flat, as though constructed in two dimensions. His raised knee fell to the side. It was his left knee. Paul saw everything clearly.

It was autumn, actually, and the leaves were sparse and brown.

The two men were climbing the hill, looking at their feet. Paul saw them. He continued walking, looking back once. The men had reached the road and were walking in the direction opposite the one Paul was walking in.

At home, Paul turned the television on and off. He poured milk into the sink, emptied the dog's dish into the garbage bag. When his parents arrived, Paul told them what he had seen.

They called the Sheriff's Office and a deputy came over. Paul told him what he had seen.

Don't tell anybody else, the deputy said. Then he went away.

Yes, he told Paul's parents when he came back, the man is where your son said he was and he is dead.

Then the deputy said, It's very important that your son

not say anything more, not to anyone. Nor should you.

They didn't, Paul and his parents. Not even to each other. Paul didn't.

He saw a dead man and the men who killed him. He never learned who the dead man was, nor who they were, nor why they killed him.

VII. What Paul's Parents Did in Georgia (II)

The restaurant became profitable at the end of its first year, an accomplishment of which Paul's parents were proud, not having expected to earn money from it until after its second year.

They bought another restaurant, this one with an established customer base, on Highway 41, across from Dobbins Air Force Base. There was a motel beside it and airmen would bring their women friends to the restaurant for a steak and then rent a room at the motel. Unlike the place Paul's parents had in the shopping center, which closed every evening after the early supper trade left, the one on the highway stayed open until midnight, its trade not only the Dobbins airmen but travelers on their way south to Miami or north to Chicago.

The patrons of the first restaurant had changed from workmen to the employees of the other stores in the center and, on weekends, the homeowners who had bought into the tracts that had recently been built in the area south of the town. The latter were settled people, or wanted to be, with young children and dreams of a safe, corporate future. The men worked for the telephone company or were air force officers or senior NCOs or worked for one or another of the manufacturing companies that were coming down from the North in search of cheap labor.

But those who came into the restaurant on the highway were not settled, though they may have been once, or may have wanted to be. Paul met a cowboy from Florida who was on his way to Arizona following a dry summer and a series of fires that had burned enough grazing land in north Florida to put him out of work. He had lived in Florida his entire life and was worried about tearing up his roots. Until Paul met him, he had not known there were cowboys in Florida.

In middle age, sitting at a table by the window in a house in a Samoan village, absorbed in the feel on his skin of the breeze coming through the window, allowing his thoughts to find their own subject, Paul would remember a man sitting at the counter over the remains of his breakfast in the restaurant on Highway 41, reading a newspaper article about the murder of a little girl in Atlanta. Paul's mother poured him another cup of coffee as a waitress swept away his plate and silverware. Paul's mother said how terrible it was about that girl and the man shrugged and said it didn't bother him.

"How can you say that?" Paul's mother demanded.

He shrugged again. "It doesn't bother me. I didn't know her. I don't know her family."

"She was just a little girl. Her family is suffering just like your family would suffer."

The man stood up. "She wasn't part of my family," he said.

"Maybe it will happen to you someday."

The man paid his bill. Paul's mother took his money and gave him his change.

"Maybe," he said.

"Are you going down to Florida?" Paul asked. He was sitting on the counter stool nearest the cash register.

The man smiled at him. "I am."

"You'll be driving through Atlanta."

The man walked outside, still smiling. When Paul turned back from watching him, his mother was staring at him. "You and your mouth," she said, and she let out a series of small, almost silent chuckles.

VIII. The Church and the Dispossessed

Before Paul's father went on leave of absence from Lockheed, Paul's family took in another family that had just moved to the United States from Germany where, it was understood but not talked about, at least in Paul's home, the husband had worked on that country's rocket program during the war. There were the husband, the wife, and a child, a girl Paul's age. It was not clear to Paul and his sister why the German family had to live with them—his sister had to give up her room and move into Paul's room with him—but they did, although only for a couple of months.

The girl was in the fourth grade with Paul. Later in his life, all Paul could recall of her was that she often farted in class, unable, or perhaps unwilling, to squeeze her farts back. With the first one, she appeared surprised that the other students laughed. After the second or third occasion, her face became inflamed and an embarrassed smile settled on it. This became her expression from then on every time she audibly passed gas.

The teacher explained that farting in class was acceptable in Germany and asked the students to be more tolerant. Some of the students tried and were even successful, but others did not try and looked forward to the next fart so they could laugh again.

After a month or two, the German couple bought a house in a different part of town and they and their daughter moved away. The girl changed schools and Paul did not see her again.

After Paul's parents became restaurant owners, when one of the elders of the Baptist Church approached them about giving a job to someone who needed one, he reminded Paul's father about what he done for the German family. From then on, when the church took in people who were down and out, it often foisted them on Paul's parents who gave them work and sometimes a place to sleep in their own house, Paul and his sister doubling up again on these occasions.

Once there was a boy and his mother. He wasn't really a boy, but Paul considered him a boy because, although he was twenty-four, he was like a playmate. In the middle of mopping the kitchen floor, he would suddenly ask if Paul wanted to play catch, or he would come over and sit next to Paul at the counter and tell him about a movie he had seen. His mother simply sat through the day, smoking cigarettes at a table in a corner, occasionally scolding her son for his laziness when she saw that Paul's parents were displeased with him. They were likable enough, especially the boy, but when they said thanks and caught the bus to move down to Florida, passed on from one Baptist congregation to another, it was wonderful to see them go.

As soon as the bus pulled away, mother and son waving to Paul's family through the window, they—Paul, his sister, and his parents—broke out laughing. It was spontaneous, and realizing this and seeing one another doubled up or gasping for breath, they laughed all the harder. They laughed until it became too painful to continue, and then they went back to the restaurant on Highway 41 and Paul swept and mopped the floor which had been one of his tasks until the boy-man took it over from him.

IX. Marv and Paul and Davy Crockett

Marv died forty-seven years after he came back from Korea and got married and came South with his bride to spend his honeymoon with Paul's family. He was Paul's favorite uncle. Paul hadn't seen him since his mother's funeral eleven years before, but he flew down to southern California to attend his. At the reception following the service, Paul enjoyed talking with Marv's children, who had suddenly become middle-aged, and other cousins he hadn't seen since they were all small. Then he flew back to

Seattle. He was surprised that he didn't feel bad.

A couple of weeks later, as Paul was driving to work, the radio started playing "Christmas in the Trenches," the song—spoken poetry, actually—about English and German soldiers getting up a soccer game in No Man's Land on Christmas Day 1914. Paul started crying; it was several minutes before he was able to stop. The sounds that were coming out of him—even though he was alone in the car, he was embarrassed. It was, of course, his losing Marv that brought on the crying. As an adult, Paul hardly saw him, but when Paul was a child, he adored Marv.

It must have been late 1950 or early 1951—it was cold enough that he had to dress heavily for warmth; this was in Chicago—that he came home from school for lunch one day and found Marv sitting on a wooden chair in the kitchen, talking with his, Paul's, mother. He was in uniform and he looked very sad or very frightened. He and Paul's mother were not joking and laughing as they usually did when they were together, but were talking soberly, just below the range of Paul's hearing. They continued talking as Paul ate, though the subject seemed to have changed. Marv left before Paul finished, hugging Paul's mother after he got into his coat and then walking out the door of the apartment, and Paul's mother began to cry. Paul didn't know what was wrong. If his mother told him, he didn't understand. This must have been just before Marv went to Korea. In middle age, Paul visualized him as he was then: not much taller than Paul's mother, skinny, with a big nose and big ears. A gangly kid. He did not have the presence that came later with size and experience.

Paul and his parents and his sister had moved South from Chicago and were living in Georgia when Marv got out of the army and got married and, not having much money, he and Marian came to stay with Paul's family for their honeymoon. Paul's mother said Marv was sick from malaria and not to expect too much from him.

Marv and Marian took a Greyhound bus down from Chicago and Paul went with his father to the bus station to pick them up. Paul and his father arrived early. It was a warm day and Paul was thirsty. He found a water fountain but there was a line of people waiting to drink from it. Wandering around, he turned a corner and found another fountain that nobody was drinking from and he went over and got water there. When he was finished, he looked up and saw an old man and woman staring at him. Then the man turned and said to Paul's father who was somewhere behind him, Paul couldn't see where, "Is this your boy?"

"Yeah, why?" Paul heard his father say. Paul had not moved from the fountain. The woman's eyes fixed him to the ground he stood on as if she had planted him there. Paul had never seen such coldness emanate from a person's face. It was entirely expressionless, as though Paul were so alien, not even something living, that there was no point in her trying to communicate with him.

"Your boy is drinking from the colored water fountain."

Paul turned back toward the fountain. When he did this, the woman took a step toward him, then stopped, apparently satisfied that he was not going to drink from it again.

Paul's father walked around from behind the man. "Did you drink from the colored water fountain?"

"No, I drank from that one." Paul pointed to it. He had no idea what his father and the large old man were talking about. When they said "colored water fountain," Paul envisioned water with colors in it. He had not seen any colors in the water he drank.

"That's the colored water fountain. There's a sign."

The old man was right. Affixed to the wall above the spout was a sign, black lettering on a white board, that read "Colored".

"The fountain for whites is over there," the old man said.

"Why did you go to that one?" Paul's father asked.

"Because there was a line at the other one. Nobody was at this one."

The three adults compared fountains. There was no one at the colored fountain; there was still a line at the whites fountain. Everybody in the line was watching the old man and woman and Paul's father and Paul.

"There was a line at this one," Paul's father said. "He didn't want to wait in line." Paul's father was smiling and there was a hint of an attempt to ingratiate in his voice.

"Didn't you see the sign?" the old man asked. His voice had softened.

"No," Paul said. He had already lived in the South long enough to know he was expected to address adult men, especially those he didn't know, as "sir," but this time he did not.

The woman's face softened a little. Paul could see that some people, in other circumstances, might think of her as kindly. He wondered which was the real person.

"He didn't see the sign," Paul's father said.

"You see a sign that says 'Colored' again, you going to drink from that fountain?" the old man said.

"No," Paul said.

"All right," the old man said. He turned to the people in the whites line. Some of them made small smiles. Others' faces remained frozen.

"Come over here, Paul," his father said. "Stay where I can see you."

When Marv and his wife stepped off the bus, Paul could see that his uncle was taller by nearly a foot than he remembered him. And although he was thin, he weighed more than two hundred pounds, Marv told him that evening.

At supper, Paul's father told Paul's mother and his uncle and aunt what happened at the bus station. Later in his life, Paul had a vague sense that Marv said something after listening to Paul's father, but Paul did not remember what it was. Marv had been a soldier in the first racially integrated army in American history. After speaking, Paul's father laughed from shame or rue for the way he had conducted himself, but he had been afraid for his son. What else could he have done? he seemed to be asking. What would have been the consequences of doing what was right?

Paul's mother, or perhaps his Aunt Marian or his uncle asked Paul if he had been afraid. He probably said no. That was how he would have answered, regardless of what he had felt, although in truth he did not remember what he said. He thought he would have denied his own fear out of consideration for his father, as well as to protect his own idea of himself. Of who he was. He was ten years old.

In middle age, Paul did not remember doing much with Marv when he was in Georgia, though he did remember their throwing a baseball back and forth, Marv catching it barehanded, as Paul did not have a glove that fit his hand, and, with Paul's father, they played pop-up. Paul worshipped him. (Paul's father, who did not have a brother, introduced Marv everywhere as "my kid brother-in-law." Paul's father did not like many people, but he liked Marv immensely.) Marv wore his hair in a pompadour and used Brill Cream to work it into the contours he wanted. Paul took up Brill Cream, but he was not able to manage a satisfactory pompadour for about three years, and by that time the ducktail and spit curl were in fashion and he had discovered petroleum jelly.

Later, Paul's sister remembered Marv and Marian buying her and Paul a Monopoly game. Until then, Paul had played chess in the evening with his father and with Marv and Marian, too, or they watched TV. Paul was very aggressive at chess and had screaming nightmares in which the chess pieces came alive and attacked his father, and perhaps Marv and Marian bought the Monopoly set in order to dampen his dreams. Or maybe they bought it so that Paul and his sister would do something together and Paul would leave Marv alone. In retrospect, Paul thought the latter was the true, or truer, explanation.

Only after Marv died did Paul realize how jealous he had been of the time Marv spent with his bride when they were with Paul and his family. He had retained memories of two kinds of emotion he felt during that time: one was adoration for Marv; the other was anger toward Marian when Marv was not paying attention to him. It must have been hard for her. Once, when he tried to butt into a conversation she and Marv were engaged in, she said to Paul, "If he had wanted you to know, he would have told you." Paul was angry enough to say something nasty in return—four and a half decades later, he didn't remember what—that hurt her.

In the early 1950s, Disney ran a TV series on Davy Crockett starring Fess Parker who, because he was so tall and seemed so sure of himself, reminded Paul of Marv. Paul loved that series and insisted that Marv watch it with him. In several of the episodes, Davy Crockett said, "Be sure you're right, then go ahead." Paul later recalled Marv telling him, as they sat side by side on the sofa after Davy spoke, "Remember that." Paul did. The difficulty in following Davy's dictum, of course, was in often not knowing what was right, or in not being able to distinguish what was right from what was self-serving.

At the dinner table, Marv belched. Paul had forgotten about his belches until, at the funeral service, one of Marv's grandchildren talked about them. Paul also had been fascinated by those belches that seemed to go on for minutes without ceasing. Could Marv really breathe and belch at the same time?

Marv began instructing him, until one evening at supper Paul sat back and crossed his arms over his chest, as Marv did his, and tried pathetically to follow Marv's lead.

Paul's parents were astounded. His father appeared not to know what to say. (But, silently, he seemed to think it was really funny.) His mother accused Marv of teaching Paul his rude habit. Marv denied it. She turned to Paul and warned him not to imitate Marv.

After supper, when Paul got him alone, he asked Marv to give him another belching lesson, but Marv declined, saying he didn't want to get Paul's mother angry at him. Once afterward, Marv belched at the table, catching the attention of Paul's parents, but apologized immediately, saying it had just slipped out.

Paul's sister reminded him, not long after Marv died, that he had had a malaria attack when he and Marian were staying with them. Paul remembered Marv being sick for a month, but malaria occurs in forty-eight-hour cycles of fever and cold and later, when Paul tried to focus his memory, he doubted that Marv was ill for more than a few days. Paul did remember Marv being isolated in one of the bedrooms and then coming out a good deal thinner and very weak. Paul remembered asking Marv to do something with him—play catch?—and Marv telling him he was too tired and then going back into the bedroom.

One afternoon Marv gave Paul his CIB—the Combat Infantryman's Badge. This is an award that is given only by the army and only to infantrymen who have been in combat. The CIB is a representation of a flintlock rifle set against a wreath, both the rifle and the wreath silver or pewter-colored, on a field of blue. It is fastened to the heart side of the dress uniform by two pins, positioned above all other awards and decorations, and sewn above the pocket on the fatigue uniform, and above the parachute wings, if the soldier has been awarded them, on the same side. Among servicemen and -women, it is highly valued, proof that its wearer has come under enemy fire. Not many soldiers see combat; most, even in an area where there is fighting, are support troops. In Korea, in the army, only one of ten or twelve was in combat.

Paul did not know why Marv gave him his CIB. He did not know what it signified to him, nor what he thought Paul would make of it. Later, Paul did not remember Marv saying anything when he handed it to him, and he was not even certain that it had happened on the brisk, sunny afternoon that he recalled Marv giving it to him, though he could, in his memory, see Marv's open hand, and see yellow sunlight coming from behind the impression Marv's body made against its background, and feel a chill again, as if it had been brought on a breeze.

In 1966, having returned from Viet Nam and needing someone to talk to, Paul went to see Marv who, a few years before, had moved out to California, following Paul's family. People who have been in war often, afterwards, find themselves searching for what is genuine in other people and have little tolerance for what is not. Paul went to see Marv because he trusted him.

They sat at the kitchen table and Marian brought them coffee. It was late morning and it was sunny on the other side of the window. Sometimes one or another of Marv's and Marian's kids would come into the kitchen with a question or to see what was going on.

Paul and Marv exchanged silly but cynical stories about their respective wars and about the army, which, for the ground soldier, seems never to change, regardless of the vaunted transformations technology purportedly brings. The pattern of the story-telling was that Paul would tell one and then Marv would match it with one from his own experience.

The last one Paul told was about a soldier whose patrol stopped for lunch. After eating, men tossed the cardboard and cans from their C-rations into the fire. Someone threw in an unopened can, which, in a moment, burst from the heat of the fire and shot jelly out in a wad, hitting Paul's friend in the mouth, burning it and splitting his lip. As the lip would not stop bleeding, he was medevac'd out of the field. Eventually he was awarded a purple heart for his wound.

Paul asked Marv about his purple heart. Paul's mother had told him that Marv had gotten it for having fallen into a foxhole and breaking a rib.

What actually happened, Marv said, was that he was trying to evade machine-gun fire and jumped into a fox-hole, breaking his rib that way. (At the reception following Marv's funeral, Paul was telling this story to Marv's children when Marian came into the room. She said that he had indeed jumped into a foxhole, but his rib was broken because he came down on another man's—a dead man's—helmet; when Marv looked, he saw that the man's face had been shot away. It was six or seven years after Marv told Paul what he wanted him to know that he told Marian what he wanted her to know.)

Swapping stories with Marv, Paul had become unsettled even as he found some of them darkly funny. Finally he was shaking so badly that he could not get the coffee to his mouth without sloshing most of it out of the cup. Marv was having the same problem. Paul had come back from war only weeks before, but Marv had been back for fourteen years. Yet his memories were apparently as vivid as Paul's. Paul did not know then that this kind of memory does not leave you, that it may sleep for a while, for years, even decades, but it is still there, waiting to surface under provocation.

They set their cups down without trying to drink any more. Marian invited Paul to stay for lunch, but he declined.

He and Marv did not talk to each other about their wars again. Neither did they talk about Davy Crockett or baseball or malaria. Later in Paul's life, he would do things that would have appalled Marv, had he known about them. But who knows what is right or wrong until things turn out badly.

X. Paul the Hero

It was the summer of the year Paul's parents bought their first restaurant. Paul's father was at his job at Lockheed after a six-month leave of absence he had taken to help get the restaurant on its feet. His mother was at the restaurant, perhaps training a cook, perhaps supervising the front.

Paul and his sister were bored. They had had enough of TV and Monopoly. Paul wanted to go outside, but his sister didn't want to be left alone, so he offered to take her on a bike ride. She could sit behind him on the seat and he would stand on the pedals. He had seen older kids ride like this. His sister did not have her own bike and their parents didn't seem in a hurry to get her one and she didn't seem in a hurry to have them buy her one. They would ride down to the end of the road where the builders hadn't put up any houses yet. It was only a hundred yards to where the asphalt turned to gravel. Beyond that was the field where Paul and his friends played baseball, though not often in the heat of the day, and beyond the field was an endless pine forest where Paul and his friends chopped down small trees with machetes their fathers and uncles had brought back from the war in the Pacific and built forts from the trees and threw pine cones and dirt clods at each other in lieu of hand grenades; it was this forest Paul would miss most when eventually he and his family left Georgia.

From the graveled turnaround, he would be able to see if Teddy or Jimmy or any of the others were playing ball. If they were, well, maybe his sister would be content to sit at the edge of the field and watch them at bat or scooping grounders.

She got on the seat and Paul straddled the ball buster, the bar that differentiated boys' bikes from girls', and put his foot on the left pedal and pushed off. He quickly found his balance and she put her arms around his middle, but his legs were pumping and she was unstable. "Hold onto the seat instead of me," Paul said, and then he didn't feel her hands on him.

Approaching the end of the street, Paul could see no one in the field. He was disappointed and decided to turn around and go back to the house.

He saw the front wheel settle into the deep gravel as he made his turn and he heard its crunch as the gravel was pushed to either side of the wheel and then the bike stopped and he worked the front wheel left and right, trying to avoid falling, and then he and his sister were lying on their left sides, entangled with the bike.

"My foot!" his sister screamed. "Don't move!"

Paul started to ease out from under the bike.

"Don't move!" his sister shrieked.

"I have to. I'll go slow. It'll just be a minute."

"A minute!"

Paul raised the bike so he could slide out from under it and was about to lay it back down when he saw that his sister's foot was wedged between the spokes of the rear wheel and that her shoe had come off and there was blood and the ankle was discolored. There was a grayish-white tone to part of it.

"I'm going to have to lift the bike off you," he said.

"Don't move it!" She tried to sit up to look at her foot, but it hurt when she moved and she winced and lay back.

"Your foot is caught in the spokes. I'm going to lay the bike down so I can bend the spokes and then you can pull your foot out."

Paul had expected her to yell again and was surprised when she said okay. She tried to raise herself on her elbows, but he said, "Don't look," and she settled back against the gravel. He saw now that there was a knot on her forehead that he hadn't noticed before, or maybe it hadn't been there. Maybe it was new.

Paul bent the spokes away that held her foot and then he bent three or four others to give her room to withdraw her foot without knocking it against one of them. He focused on the discoloration of her ankle and realized he was looking at the bone. All the skin had been scraped off.

She withdrew her foot from the wheel without making a sound. She didn't try to sit up.

Paul scanned the nearest houses to see if there were cars in the driveways. He didn't know everybody on the street. Some people had only recently moved in and he didn't know their routines. He didn't see any cars.

"What are you doing?" his sister asked.

"I'm trying to figure out if there's somebody around to help us."

"Don't leave me!"

"I won't. I'm going to squat down next to you and I want you to reach up and put your arms around my neck and then I'm going to put my arm behind your knees and I'm going to stand up so I'll be carrying you in my arms." A year earlier a fireman had visited his class and shown the kids some things firemen did when they rescued people. This was one of the techniques Paul remembered, or it was a variation on one of the techniques. Paul didn't think he could flip his sister over his shoulder or swing her around so she could ride on his back horsey style, not with her ankle the way it was. When he lifted her, he watched her face for an indication of pain. He didn't see any, but the knot on her forehead was larger. He started walking.

"Where are we going?"

"Home."

"Can you carry me that far?"

"Yes. Be quiet now."

He was trying to save his breath. He paid attention to the way her arms felt on his neck. He was worried about the lump on her head and he was afraid she might pass out.

His arms started to ache and then, after a while, he lost sensation in them, but he didn't set her down and he kept walking. He realized he had learned something: you can do what you don't think you can do if you ignore how bad it feels.

In their house again, Paul laid his sister down on the sofa in the living room. He told her to lie back so he could look at the knot on her forehead again. He thought there was a greater possibility of the knot turning into something terrible than there was for her ankle, but he also didn't want her to see how bad her ankle looked. He went into the kitchen and ran a dishcloth under the cold water from the tap and then he took some ice cubes out of the tray in the freezer and folded the dishcloth around them and returned to the living room where he placed the cold cloth on his sister's forehead.

"Hold that there."

"What's wrong?" she asked, but she did as he told her.

"There's some swelling. The ice will bring it down. I'll be right back."

He went back in the kitchen and made another compress, but without ice cubes. The purpose of this one was to conceal the wound on her ankle from her. He laid the cool cloth on her ankle after warning her it might sting, though it seemed not to.

"Where did you learn to do that?"

"I don't know," Paul said. "In another life. I was a doctor."

"Really?"

They had talked sometimes about reincarnation, whether it was true or not, and what kind of person each of them would have liked to have been. They played with the notion once that they might have been different animals altogether, but they discarded that idea because they didn't know enough about other animals to be able to imagine what it would be like to live as one of them.

"Sure," Paul said.

"What was your name?"

"I'm teasing you," he said. He didn't have the energy to make something up and sustain it.

"Is it bad?" his sister asked.

"Is what bad?"

"My foot."

"No. We just have to wait until Dad gets home."

He visualized his father coming in the kitchen door about four o'clock. Paul would have to leave his sister and go into the kitchen to tell his father what happened before he saw her. His father could be impulsive and Paul had seen him lapse into irrationality a couple of times, and he could infect other people with his fears or his anger. Paul saw his job now as keeping his sister calm. He was doing it pretty well, he thought, and he didn't want his father upsetting her and wrecking his work.

She had dozed off and Paul thought that might be dangerous, given her head injury. He raised the cloth from her forehead. The swelling had not worsened and he thought it might even have gone down a little. He didn't wake her. He took her hand and held it without squeezing it.

He heard the doorknob rattle in the kitchen. He glanced at the face on the grandfather clock. His father was early. He let go of his sister's hand and she opened her eyes.

"It's Dad," Paul said.

He went into the kitchen. His father was just coming through the doorway, talking over his shoulder to another man. The other man was a little taller than Paul's father and wore glasses. Like Paul's father, he had on a white, short-sleeve shirt and a tie and a pen protector in his shirt pocket. Paul assumed he was someone his father knew from his job. His father left off what he was saying and began to introduce Paul to his friend, but Paul said, "There's been an accident but it's not serious and Bonnie's been hurt…"

"What! Where is she?"

Paul could see the panic in his father's eyes. Something fell out of his father's hand to the floor.

"In the living room, but it's not serious…"

His father moved past him, the other man following.

"Oh my god!" Paul heard his father shout. Paul caught

up with him. His father had removed the cloth from his sister's ankle and she looked from her father to Paul and Paul said, "It's not serious," and his sister began to wail.

"What's this?" Paul's father asked, pointing at the compress on his sister's forehead.

"She had a bump on her head. I was trying to get the swelling down."

His father pulled the cloth away. Before he could say "Oh my god" again, Paul said, "It's gone down. It was worse."

"How'd it happen?"

"We were on my bike…"

"Both of you?"

"You should call your doctor, Herb," the other man put in. Paul's father dashed into the kitchen and Paul heard him pick up the phone from its cradle on the wall.

"Am I going to die?" his sister asked.

"No, you're not going to die. You know how he is."

"Are you sure?"

"I guarantee it. If you go, I'll go too."

"How will you do it?"

"How will I do what?"

"How will you kill yourself? How will I know you're dead if I'm already dead?"

"Jesus, Bonnie."

"You guaranteed. How will I know you didn't lie to me? You lied to me before."

"I did not. When?"

"You said it wasn't serious. I believed you."

"You haven't died, have you? So it's not serious."

"Fuck you, Paulie."

He was shocked. She had never said that to him before. He had never heard her use that word. Where had she learned it? Oh. She had probably heard him and Teddy talking.

His father was back. "We're going to meet the doctor at the hospital," he said to his friend, as though his friend were a part of all this. To Paul, his father said, "I want you to stay here in case your mother calls. I had to leave her a message, but if she calls here, tell her I took Bonnie to the hospital and tell her what happened." He stared at Paul. "What happened?" he asked.

"We'd better get going, Herb. Traffic is going to get worse."

Paul's father scooped his sister up from the couch without warning and Paul saw her face squeeze shut with pain or the fear of it.

"Are you going to be all right?" the other man asked.

Paul nodded.

"You did a good job," the man said.

As they were leaving the house, Paul heard him tell his father, "I'll drive."

It took a while to get used to the silence in the house and in his mind. Paul sat down on the sofa and waited for his mother to call.

After a while he decided that his mother wasn't going to call and he walked down the road to where his bike lay and brought it home. A couple of cars pulled into their driveways as Paul walked. People were getting home from work.

When Paul's parents and sister came back from the hospital, Paul's father asked him, "Did you knock Bonnie off your bike on purpose?"

Paul glared at his sister who was lying on the couch again.

"You were trying to make me fall off! You were twisting the bike all around!" she shouted.

XI. Sixth Grade

Paul had a teacher for the sixth grade, Mrs. Hawes, who was from New York. Like Paul's father, her husband had gotten a job in the defense industry and Mrs. Hawes had moved to Georgia with him. It was she who told the children in Paul's class that southern schools were to be integrated next year. She explained what that meant. Most of the children did not know that black kids and white kids were prohibited from attending the same school. The kids in Paul's class did not see black kids in their daily lives, so did not think about them. If they were to think of them, they would have assumed that black kids attended a different school because they lived in a different part of town.

The only black person the children in Paul's class saw on a daily basis was Mr. Brown, the school janitor, a reserved, older man who never lost his composure. When Mrs. Hawes told the children in Paul's class why school integration had been ordered and how black people had been treated for so long, some of the girls began to cry. They had had no idea. After school they found Mr. Brown in the hallway and gathered around him, sobbing. Mr. Brown did not lose his composure. He smiled in sympathy with their tears, careful not to touch any of them. His eyes showed utter bewilderment.

XII. Boy Scouts

Jimmy, Paul's scoutmaster, had been born in Georgia but had lived in the North. He had lived in Chicago and had gone to some of the same nightclubs Paul's parents talked about. He had been a bouncer at the Chez Paree, Paul's father's favorite club, but they had not known each other there. After he was a bouncer at the Chez Paree, Jimmy was in the Air Force. This was during the Korean War. He had taught airmen hand-to-hand combat. He was an expert in judo. Out with his scout troop during overnight camp-outs, he would sometimes wrestle two or three boys at the same time, one arm tied behind his back. He always defeated them. Jimmy was not Paul's uncle Marv; Paul did not worship him, but he almost did.

When Jimmy returned to Georgia after his years away, he worked at a number of jobs that held no meaning for him. This was when he became a scoutmaster. It was in his capacity as Paul's scoutmaster that he met Paul's father. Eventually he asked Paul's father if he would recommend him for a job at Lockheed, and Paul's father did.

Paul's father liked Jimmy and his wife, and occasionally they would come over to Paul's house for dinner. Once,

sitting in the living room after supper, the grown-ups talked about what was going to happen next year. Although
Jimmy's kids were small, not yet old enough to go to
school, he was concerned. Eventually they would go to
school and he did not want them to go to school with Negro kids. Paul thought it was interesting that Jimmy never
used the words "nigger" or "nigra," but still expressed prej-
udicial feelings.

Either Paul's mother or his father asked why not and
Jimmy said he just didn't. He was all for Negroes being
equal to whites, he did not mind that at all, but he did
not want their children going to school with his children.
Paul's parents tried to get him to tell them why he didn't,
but he seemed unable. This was the last time Jimmy and
his wife came over to Paul's house, or one of the last times.
Things began to move very fast soon afterward and Paul
did not see much of him again.

In fact, he saw Jimmy now as a little tarnished. Blem-
ished. After that evening, he separated himself from Jimmy a little. It was not something he intended, but he
found himself listening less to what Jimmy said, no longer
seeking him out after scout meetings to talk with him.
And then Jimmy was gone. The demands of his job, the
overtime—he no longer had the time for scouting.

Someone else took Jimmy's place in the troop. Under
the new leadership, scouting became more formal. You
were penalized if you missed a meeting without an acceptable excuse, and you were penalized if you did not
wear your uniform to meetings or if your uniform was not
complete or if you did not snap your salute. Scouting had

become militarized, though Paul did not know enough then to have expressed it that way. He had liked scouting when it was fun, but he did not like it now. He stopped attending the meetings.

XIII. On Highway 41

Once a bus filled with soldiers pulled up in front of the restaurant on Highway 41. As the soldiers filed inside, the staff got busy. Until he walked in, no one noticed that one of the soldiers, the second or third from the end, was black. But then the cashier saw him and she got Paul's father.

Paul's father came out from the back of the restaurant and explained to the soldiers that the law prohibited him from serving black people where white customers ate. He was apologetic and, seeing his face, Paul believed he was ashamed of what he was doing. Paul's father said he could serve the black soldier in the kitchen or he could bring his order to him on the bus.

The black soldier understood. He appeared to appreciate Paul's father's dilemma and the humiliation he was suffering. Paul's father, for his part, seemed on the verge of laughing hysterically or breaking into tears.

Several of the white soldiers were angry and did not try to conceal their anger. They talked of simply going somewhere else to eat, but then realized that wherever they might go in the South, they would run into the same situation. They accused Paul's father and the cashier and a waitress—all the restaurant help they could see—of racial prejudice, focusing particularly on Paul's father because they recognized from his accent that he was from the North. For a moment or two, Paul thought they might attack his father or try to wreck the restaurant and the coppery taste of adrenalin filled his mouth.

Finally, while some soldiers sat down at the counter or at tables, others had their orders dished onto paper picnic plates and they took these into the bus and ate there with the black soldier.

After they ate, as Paul and his father collected the trash from the bus and stuffed it into paper bags, some of the soldiers apologized for the things they had said, while making it clear that they believed they were in the right, and that, if not Paul's father personally and the cashier and everyone in the restaurant they had abused, the South was fucked up.

Paul's father apologized again to the black soldier and the soldier said it was all right, he understood.

XIV. How Paul and His Family Came to Georgia and How They Left

1

Paul looked out the window while Mommy fixed supper. The snow was all black in the street where the cars ran over it, but on the sidewalk it was still white. It was squishy in the street but it was squeaky on the sidewalk. He wanted to go outside but Mommy said it was too cold out and it was getting dark now and anyway supper would be ready soon.

Paul was not hungry but Mommy insisted. We'll eat early before Daddy gets home, said Mommy. We'll play a trick on Daddy. Paul wanted to eat with Daddy but he liked tricks, so he said, All right, but who are you going to eat with? I'll eat a little bit with you and a little bit with Daddy when he gets home, Mommy said. So Paul ate even though he was not hungry and Mommy ate just a little bit.

After a while Daddy came home, looking very tired. He had to ride forty-five minutes on the El to work and forty-five minutes on the El from work, and the two rides and the crowding and the constant voices in so many different tones and inflections and the jostling and poking in addition to whatever happened at work made him tired.

At work, where he worked on things for the government that he couldn't talk about, people respected him. He was a star, Paul had heard one of the men his father worked with say one evening when the man and his wife were eating supper with Paul's parents. Paul's father was confident that he would rise from where he was in his life. Paul heard his father say that, or something like that, later that night.

When Daddy came home Mommy was very nice to him and told him that dinner was ready and Daddy was hungry and he and Mommy sat down at the table. But then Daddy asked, Why wasn't Paul eating? And because it was a trick, Paul answered, Because I don't want to, that's why. Because it was a trick he made his voice very snotty-like, as if he were bigger than his father.

Daddy got up so fast that Paul could not think, and he could not think either because of the horrible expression on Daddy's face. And Daddy grabbed Paul and picked him up and shook him up and down, up and down, up and down, bouncing Paul's feet on the sofa, and Paul could feel something inside his head shaking around and his teeth were hitting against each other and something inside his stomach was jiggling around too. And Mommy was sitting at the table eating her dinner with her fork very slowly, and Daddy was shouting.

Later Paul heard Mommy telling Daddy that it had all been a trick and Daddy came into Paul's room where Paul was in bed because of his stomach and all the bouncing, and Daddy said he was sorry and Paul could see that Daddy was and said, 'That's okay, Daddy, you just didn't give me a chance to explain, and Paul felt his throat get choky. He saw that Daddy felt that way too, and in his eyes too. And Daddy said, I know, and they kissed goodnight like they did every night and Daddy went out and everything was all right again.

2

Something was wrong. It was nighttime but the doctor was here. Paul recognized his voice even though he couldn't hear well enough to know what the doctor was saying. He climbed out of bed and went into the front room. The doctor said the word "tonight." When Paul went into the front room he thought his parents would be angry with him for being out of bed so late. He didn't mean to go into the front room, he had meant only to listen at the door, but he hadn't been able to hear very well and then the door opened somehow and he found himself in the room with his mother and father and the doctor.

His mother's and father's faces looked strange. He could not understand what their faces were saying to him. The doctor looked strange too.

"Get your clothes on," his father said. "Get dressed."

"What's wrong?" Paul asked.

"Help him get dressed," his mother said to his father. She was crying, not with her whole face but with only her eyes.

"What's wrong?"

His father was taking him to his aunt's house. His mother had taken his sister and gone with the doctor. His sister was sick. She was going to the hospital. No, she wasn't going to die, his father said. She was just sick and she would have to stay in the hospital for a while. She would have to have an operation. It was nothing serious. Paul would have to stay with his aunt for a while, for a few days, for a week or two. He could go to school with his cousin. He liked his cousin, didn't he? And he liked his aunt?

He liked his aunt but he didn't like the way she smelled. She smelled stale, like old milk, as if somebody had forgotten to drink her and she was still sitting in a glass on the table. She gave him milk and cookies to eat while she talked with his father.

When his father left, she smiled at him. He knew she was trying to make him feel less lonely. But he didn't like her anymore. He poured the rest of his milk in the sink.

His sister was in a big crib with four little tricycle wheels. She looked dopey. She was all doped up, his father said. She didn't know anything. She just looked at him. She had plastic tubes sticking out of her arms and legs.

"Say hello to your sister," his mother told him.

"Hi," Paul said.

His sister just looked at him.

"Hi," Paul said again. "Can she hear me?" he asked his father.

"She probably hears you," the doctor said. The doctor was standing next to his father. This was a new doctor. The old doctor had died. Of a heart attack.

"But she can't say anything," Paul said. He said it as a matter of fact, as something he had observed.

"She'll be able to talk to you tomorrow. She's not feeling very good right now."

The nurse wheeled her away. To her room, his father said.

"Goodbye," Paul said.

Paul and his father and mother drove home. It had been a long time since they had driven home in the car together. Usually it was just Paul and his father. It felt different with his mother in the car now. It felt nice but it felt different.

"What do you think?" his father asked.

"About what?" said his mother.

"About moving."

"Do we have a choice? The doctor said another winter in Chicago would kill her." His mother began to cry.

"How would you like to move to Georgia?" Paul's father asked him.

"I don't want to," Paul said.

"It's warm there all year round. And they have big juicy peaches there. Georgia peaches. Haven't you ever heard of Georgia peaches?"

"I don't want to. I'll never see Mickey and Danny and Jimmy and Bobby again if we go there."

"You'll see them again," his mother said.

"How?" Paul demanded.

"They can visit us in Georgia."

"They won't. I'll never see them again."

"We don't have a choice," his mother said. She was crying again. She had never been out of Chicago except to her parents' cottage on the Fox River. Paul's father had once lived in California.

3

Paul lived with his parents and sister in Georgia in a town called Marietta. His third-grade teacher told the class that Marietta was named for the two daughters, Mary and Etta, of one of the founding fathers of the town, a man whose name was Cobb. Marietta was the seat of Cobb County. Inscribed in the frontal stone of the courthouse was "Reconstructed 1868." The teacher said that before The War Between The States one hundred thousand people lived in Marietta. Marietta had been bigger than Atlanta. But General Sherman burned Marietta on his March To The Sea. Now only twenty thousand people lived in Marietta, and it was smaller than Atlanta.

Paul's fifth-grade teacher said that if the schools were integrated nigras would go to school with white students and would be in the same classrooms. Paul thought that "nigras" meant Negros but he wasn't sure. He couldn't always understand what his teacher said. It had been more than a year before he recognized that "all" could mean "all" or "awl" or "oil." Paul understood what "nigger" meant, and that his parents did not permit him to say that word, but he had never heard anyone say "nigra" until now. He thought maybe his teacher could say "Negro" but didn't want to.

4

Paul's parents owned a restaurant outside of town on Highway 41 and employed as a cook a Negro whose name was Chuck. Chuck was a fine cook, an excellent cook, and Paul's parents and his sister and he liked him personally, but he lived in Tacoa and he didn't own a car. This meant that he had to rely on his friends to drive him to work and to pick him up afterward, so that he was often late going in either direction. Because he had such a talent for cooking, a rare thing in Marietta's restaurant establishments, Paul's father decided to buy him a car, an older car, inexpensive but reliable.

Paul and his father went to a lot in Tacoa where his

father picked out a sky-blue Chevy that met his require-
ments, leaving the car in the lot until he deposited money enough into his account to pay the whole amount by
check. Paul's father, a child of the Depression, distrusted
credit; he despised the idea of being owned by anyone.

Two days later Chuck called from his home and asked
Paul's father to hurry up to Tacoa to pay for the car because those men who owned the car lot were crazy. It was
not clear what was going on or how they were crazy.

As he and his father pulled into the lot, Paul noticed a
two-by-four plank with two nails sticking out of it at one
end. He thought that someone should move it before a car
ran over it and punctured a tire. When he got out of the
car, he started to go over and pick it up with the idea of
tossing it out of the way of where cars might drive, but his
father was already going inside and Paul went after him.
He made a mental note to move the board before they left
the lot.

The car lot was owned by two brothers. One of them
had a very fat, thick neck. The other was smaller, with a
throat that made small pimples against the razor's pull.
When Paul's father stepped into the office, the larger
brother said, "Mr. Donaldson, why didn't you tell us you
were buying this car for a nigger?"

Before Paul's father could say anything, or perhaps he
did say something, this brother, the big one, the one with
the thick, sweating neck and red-meat fists, slammed into
him. The other brother, the one with the scrawny, stubbly
throat, slid behind Paul's father and either held him back
or kept him from falling, Paul couldn't be certain which.

It was over very fast. After a minute, or maybe less, the larger brother stepped away and the smaller brother let go of Paul's father's arms and Paul's father rolled across the floor with his knees drawn up. There was quite a lot of noise in Paul's ears and when the big and little brothers turned toward him wearing expressions of startle or surprise on their faces, Paul realized that he had been screaming and swearing hysterically throughout the beating. He became aware, too, that he held in his hands the two-by-four plank with the two nails in it; he didn't remember having run outside to get it, though clearly he must have.

The two brothers were staring at him. The smaller one started toward him and Paul raised the board as though to smash him with it and he moved back.

"Mr. Donaldson, tell your son to put the board down," one of the brothers said.

Paul's father did tell him this, but Paul refused because he did not trust these men not to hit his father again once they could do it without incurring harm to themselves. Finally the two brothers convinced him that they would not hit his father any more and Paul turned and threw the board outside. On the floor was a fair amount of blood and teeth. The bigger brother turned to Paul's father who was on one knee now, and said quietly but loudly, "We don't like you damned Yankees coming down here and telling us how to run our affairs."

Paul and his father drove back to the restaurant to tell Paul's mother what had happened and that they would be going to the courthouse to inform the District Attorney of what had happened and to begin the process that would obtain either justice or revenge. Paul's father pulled into a parking stall, then sent Paul inside alone because he did not want people to see him looking as he did. It took Paul a while to convince his mother to come outside. She thought his father was playing a joke on her, getting her to come outside and then somehow tricking her, and she was not in a frame of mind to entertain jokes. She had her own news.

A waitress followed her out, perhaps to defend her against Paul's father's trick, perhaps not. Perhaps she was the one Paul's father had slept with; perhaps she was trying to control the flow of information. The waitress understood first that something bad had happened and she returned to the doorway to observe from there. Later, when Paul remembered this scene, he was both at the doorway, standing beside her, observing his parents, and also standing beside the car, watching and listening to them speak.

Paul's mother did not seem to know what to think. First her face did one thing, then it did another. On it was surprise, then humor, then surprise again—all of this before she or Paul's father said a word. She did not give her news then. Later, Paul did not remember her saying anything at this point. On the other hand, he remembered his father opening the door to get out of the car and his mother insisting that he not. So maybe she did tell him what happened and maybe his impulse was to go and look, and maybe she told him it could wait.

When Paul's father told her he was going to see the District Attorney, she tried to talk him out of it. She wanted him to forget that he had been beaten up. "Just forget about it," she said. Of course he could not. Paul's father wanted justice or revenge. He wanted it all never to have happened, but he was not able to deny that it had.

Homer Holmes was the District Attorney of Cobb County. He had a fine leather office in the courthouse in Marietta. Waiting with his father in the corridor to see Homer Holmes, Paul couldn't keep his eyes from a girl with straw-and-sand hair who was breast-feeding her baby; she was not much older than he was. Many other people were in the corridor and they couldn't take their eyes off of Paul's father.

The District Attorney had a thick, sweaty neck and large meat-and-knuckle hands. He placed Paul's father under "technical arrest" for disturbing the peace of the public by presenting himself openly with such a face. He told Paul's father to go home and to remain there until notified that he could leave. The District Attorney was a cousin by blood to the two brothers in Tacoa whose business it was to sell used cars.

The neighbors from across the street were gentle, slow-speaking people from Alabama. They came to visit, sympathize, advise. The husband shook his head sadly and said, "Herb, you shouldn't have got involved in our affairs." The wife had a dead grandfather who had lost a leg in The War Between The States.

Paul passed his twelfth birthday fishing on the Chattahoochee River. Evenings, he bussed and washed dishes in his parents' restaurant. On occasion he locked himself in the bathroom where he would rehearse jab and cross, finishing with a blood-splattering haymaker. Afterward he would sweat and breathe heavily and deeply and he would run cold water on his wrists to calm himself and take the flush from his face.

He would be six feet six inches tall.

He would be broad but lean and have sledge fists.

He would concentrate steel hatred into lethal shafts directed from his eyes.

5

Paul's father retained a lawyer. The lawyer was a young, sandy-haired man whose office was in the front part of the house he shared with his mother and sister. He had a reputation for being honest.

Paul's father said he was going to get his cousins to come down from Chicago and take revenge on the two brothers in Tacoa. Paul's father had grown up in Chicago during some very tough times and Paul knew he had cousins who had been gangsters, but he doubted that his father would call them.

"Don't talk like that," the lawyer said. "You can be angry, but you'll only make things worse if you go around saying things like that."

The lawyer asked if Paul would be able to testify in court about what he saw. Paul would be a credible witness because of his age. Paul said he could do it.

On a rack beside the cash register postcards were displayed for sale. On one was a cartoon drawing showing an office door with an opaque glass window. Depicted as a shadow on the window was a man sucking a woman's breast. On the doorknob hung a sign that said "Out To Lunch."

Homer Holmes, the District Attorney of Cobb County, determined that Paul's parents were selling pornographic literature and came with the Sheriff to close down the restaurant. While the District Attorney was announcing his intention to Paul's parents, Paul asked the Sheriff if he and the District Attorney were in the Ku Klux Klan. The Sheriff made a small smile. "No," he said.

The people who owned the motel next to the restaurant offered to buy it for a price only a little less than what Paul's parents thought the restaurant was worth. The people who owned the motel were attractive, gracious people who had a daughter whom Paul had liked. She had dark hair, darker than Paul's own, and a blotchless complexion. She had a self-knowing, comforting way of speaking, as though all things, even the saddest things, were inevitable and must be endured. Paul had liked her very much.

The leader of the Baptist Church in town saw Paul and his father one day on the street and came over to them. Paul was surprised that the Baptist leader did not pretend he hadn't seen them. "I'm sorry this happened to you, Mr. Donaldson," he said, as though things happen to people inexplicably and it was always sad when they did. He was dismayed that Paul's parents had sold their restaurant on Highway 41, but he knew, of course, that they had sold the one in the shop-

ping center, what was it? a year ago now? He smiled at
Paul.

Paul's father's lawyer said he wasn't going to have Paul testify. Because of his age, the lawyer said, he wouldn't be a
credible witness.

Paul's father stared at the lawyer.

So, without your son's testimony, we don't have a case.

You're not going to let him testify, Paul's father said.

No, the lawyer said. That's true, I'm not, he added to
be certain Paul's father understood.

Paul's father stared.

I live here, the lawyer said.

Many of Paul's mother's family had moved to California
from Chicago. Paul's father used to live there, in California. Now he had a job in the aircraft industry in Los
Angeles. Only a month after the people who owned the
motel next door made the offer to buy the restaurant Paul,
with his parents and sister, began the drive to California.

6

Paul went to school with his cousin. Paul's cousin liked
to pick fights with other kids and then run to find Paul.
Paul fought almost every day, even though he was always
afraid. His cousin never fought.

On Saturdays Paul went to the movies with his cousin

and his sister when she was well enough. One movie was a gangster movie. It starred Richard Conte as a gangster who was betrayed. Richard Conte looked like Paul's father. There were many killings and beatings in the movie and Paul could not watch these scenes when they showed men bleeding. When Richard Conte was killed at the end of the movie, Paul could not watch that scene.

At school a gang of boys surrounded Paul and pushed him around. They told him his mother fucked dogs and blew sailors. They said he didn't know who his father was, and his mother couldn't be sure. They told him they were going to drag him off to the boys' toilet and make him eat shit. There were eight or ten in the gang and other kids stopped to watch. Girls were watching and one who was Paul's friend was angry with him for allowing himself to be humiliated. When the bell rang the ringleader punched Paul in the stomach and Paul went down. He stayed down while the ringleader and others called back demeaning things as they left for class. The ringleader's name was Willy.

Paul caught Willy in the bathroom and broke Willy's nose. Paul caught Willy again and bloodied his mouth. Paul caught one of Willy's friends and made him drink water out of the toilet. Paul caught another of Willy's friends and hit him with a trash can lid until he couldn't get up. Paul had steel taps put on his shoes. He caught another one of Willy's friends and kicked his legs until the boy cried. Paul was always afraid, even when he slept, and when finally Willy moved away to Texas and Paul didn't see either Willy or his friends anymore, he felt wonderfully relieved.

Paul had a friend named George who was very large but very nice. Paul's parents called him "the gentle giant." One day, Paul's father asked him if he thought he could beat up George. Paul wanted to say no, but he said instead, "I don't know." Finally he said, "I think I can."

He would be six feet six inches tall.

He would have sledge fists.

He would concentrate steel hatred in his eyes.

It didn't hurt. He thought it would, but even as he struck himself he knew that at worst he was raising a few lumps, he wasn't punching out his teeth or breaking the bones in his face. It was strange: even through the self-beating he was able to think, to gauge the effect on his father. Yet the rage was real: the redness of it!

After Paul stopped crying he lay exhausted on the bed. His father left him then, and Paul heard his steps leading into the kitchen where his aunt and uncle and cousin were with his mother and sister. "He was hitting himself," Paul heard his father say. Bewilderment was in his voice.

Paul's cousin appeared at the bedroom door. "Can I come in?"

"Yes."

"They're eating now."

"I'm not hungry."

"I'm not either. I ate a whole turkey leg and part of the other one before your sister saw me."

Paul laughed.

"How come you were hitting yourself?"

Paul said nothing.

"You don't look like you hit yourself very hard."

"He didn't even hit them back!"

"What?"

"When they were beating him, he didn't even fight back! He didn't hit them once! He didn't even try!"

"He said he was afraid of what they would do to you."

"He didn't even try!"

"Maybe you should go to sleep now."

Paul hoped that his father had heard him shouting. He hated his father.

Paul's father sat down on the edge of the bed. It was almost dark now. Paul did not remember sleeping.

"When those two gorillas were hitting me, all I could think about was you. Do you remember yelling at them to leave me alone?"

"I remember screaming. I don't remember what I was saying."

"Do you remember what they said?"

"No."

"They told me that if you didn't put the board down they would beat you up too."

"It wasn't my fault!" Paul screamed.

He was crying. It was something he couldn't control. His chest hurt so much it frightened him. "I love you, Daddy," he managed to get out from the constriction of his throat.

"I love you too, Paulie," his father said, holding him.
He would be six feet six.
He would have sledge fists.

"Well, what do you think?" Paul's father asked.
"I don't care what you do," said Paul's mother.
"It would mean more money."
"Do whatever you want."
The corporation Paul's father worked for had offered
him a vice-presidency contingent on his joining a society
that stood against Communism, Negroes, and Jews, and
made clandestine campaign contributions to particular
political candidates. All of the corporation's vice-presi-
dents were members of that society, Paul's father said.
And Paul's sister was sick. That had to be considered; there
were going to be expenses, even with the insurance.
"Do whatever you want," Paul's mother said again.

Paul's father said, "They ought to hang them from lamp
poles, teach the bastids a lesson."
"Who?" Paul asked.
"The niggahs!"
Paul lived with his parents and sister in a sprawling
frame house in Orange County. There were three bedrooms and a den, a living room, a dining room, a kitchen
with all the conveniences, a recreation room, two bath-
rooms, a four-car garage, a wishing well in the front yard,
fruit trees in the back, and three-quarters of an acre of

lawn and shrubs surrounding. Paul's father commuted from affluence to work every day. Evenings and weekends, he puttered. Paul's sister was very often ill. His mother watched television.

Paul's father had a heart attack one day while at work. No damage was done to the heart, the doctor said, which was unusual, considering the symptoms, but the symptoms were real enough. Paul's father experienced his second heart attack at the entrance to the corporate campus immediately upon his return to work after recovering from the symptoms of the first. The symptoms of the second killed him.

At his father's funeral a ruddy, thick-waisted man who had worked with his father told Paul how tragic it was that Herb in the prime of his life should be killed in a freeway accident. "It makes no sense," said the red-faced man.

Paul would be six feet six inches tall upon his return.

He would be broad but lean and have sledge fists.

He would concentrate steel hatred into lethal shafts directed from his eyes.

He wouldn't. He couldn't.

He would never go back.

Amplification: Something Else that Happened on the Day of the Beating and What Paul's Mother May Not Have Told His Father

On the day of the beating Paul's father intended to work in the back room of the restaurant—the banquet room, which was open to customers only in the evening. Taxes would be due soon and he and Paul would work on their preparation together. Paul would go through the receipts and recite the numbers and his father would punch them into the adding machine. His father could do both tasks without Paul, of course, and more efficiently—Paul would have questions about particular receipts and his father would have to stop his fingers' working in order to answer them: There are different amounts on this one: which did he want? The print on this one is so light I can't read it—but, as was the case with lawn work, gardening, and erecting a fence around their backyard, he wanted Paul's company.

They had set the adding machine and paper and pencils and some ledgers on one of the tables when Chuck called. Something was wrong, he told Paul's father. The men he was buying the car from were crazy and he needed to get over to the lot right away. Paul's father had planned to pick up the car on the following day, but because of the fear in Chuck's voice he decided to go now. Paul went with him. There was no reason why he should not; they were going to spend the day together anyway. And so they went to Tacoa and Paul's father was beaten and ultimately Paul and his father and mother and sister left Georgia. Paul's father never learned—at least he never told Paul—what the men who owned the car lot told Chuck to frighten him so.

But he learned something else, possibly when he and Paul returned to the restaurant, or perhaps later. Between the time his father and Paul left for Tacoa and the beating that awaited them, and the time of their return to the restaurant, something happened that Paul's mother wanted to tell his father about when they returned. A car had turned off the highway and driven through the brick wall of the banquet room and into the room itself, massing tables, chairs, and all else that was before it against the far wall in a porcupine jumble of planes and spines, table tops and chair seats and the legs from all of them. When one of the cooks went back to turn off the ignition, the rear tires were still milling against the floor tiles. Paul saw these tiles the next day, their surfaces scorched black. Paul's father pointed them out to him.

The driver of the car was dead. The police told Paul's parents the next day. He apparently had had a heart attack while at the wheel and died immediately as the car swerved off the road. The police found his body on the floorboards. The cook who turned off the ignition had not noticed it or, if he had, did not say anything about it.

In later years Paul's mother used to say that maybe it was all for the best: if Paul's father and he had stayed to work on the taxes, both of them would have been killed.

Paul's father's response was that God could have gotten them out of the banquet room without sending them to Tacoa. Paul himself did not feel grateful to God.

Paul's father seldom referred to the beating he received as what it was—a beating. He alluded to it elliptically, if he alluded to it at all, or simply left the allusion unsaid, knowing that Paul's mother, his sister and Paul understood what he did not want to say.

Addendum

Twenty-one years after Homer Holmes drove Paul's family from Georgia, Paul was working in Seattle as Chief of Security at Providence Hospital. This was shortly before Providence began renovating to become the medical center it is now. At the information desk just inside the main entrance sat a woman who volunteered at the hospital two or three times a week. On this day Paul saw sorrow on her face and he asked what was wrong. Her daughter's father-in-law had died this morning during open-heart surgery, she said. Her daughter and her husband would be flying out to Georgia for the funeral. It was terribly sad. He had been an admirable man, and still young.

"Where in Georgia?" Paul asked.

"Marietta. It's a small city near Atlanta. He was the District Attorney there."

"I used to live there."

"Really? How odd that we should be talking today. When did you live there?"

"Oh, a long time ago. I was a little boy."

"Well, perhaps you heard of him. He was the District Attorney for years and years. His name was Homer Holmes."

After a moment Paul said, "I knew him. My family knew part of his."

"Really! And we're talking today, three thousand miles away from where he died, and we both knew him. When did you last see him?"

"I left Marietta over twenty years ago."

"Still, how strange it is that you knew him and that we're here now, talking about him. The world really is very small. Would you mind if I gave my daughter your name and told her about our conversation?"

"I don't mind. But it's my father's name that the Holmes family may remember." Paul told her his father's name. "Or they may not."

Paul called his mother that night and told her that Homer Holmes had died and how he knew. She said, simply, "Good."

Paul's mother died twelve years later. It was then, in the weeks before she died, that she told Paul of his father's infidelity. Paul did not know until she told him that his father had fallen in love with one of the waitresses who worked for them. His mother did not tell Paul when she found out; Paul did not think she knew on the day his father was beaten up, the day she and the waitress who, Paul now suspected, was his father's lover rushed out of the restaurant to learn what had befallen him. Paul did not know when she found out, but it was soon after he and his family arrived in California that he noticed his parents' estrangement from each other.

In the days before his mother died, more and more of her feeling about his father came out, until Paul thought that she hated him more deeply than she had loved him, that by the time he died she may not have loved him at all.

She accused Paul, too, of having betrayed her, although she did not say in what way.

Paul's sister is well for now. She has encountered one malady after another and she has fought them off, though not without residual damage. It seems that once one thing in the body goes out of harmony, other things follow.

Life proceeds by indirection.

AMBITION

Thirty something, forty something—how can you tell nowadays? So attractive, so spare in that raw, corporate way are these assistant professors. She is bitter about the hurdles she must jump in order to advance her career. "Sometimes you have to do things you don't want to do," she complains.

We are in the garden behind her chairman's house. Roses, trellis-bound, send a heavy, tropical scent into the moist air, excite a faint sexuality. One of us, a friend of the chairman's nephew, asks if she would send blacks to concentration camps if her dean told her to and if she had the power. He asks in search of a limit, a boundary she will not cross. It is conversation. We are discussing abstractions. Soon we will all go inside for dinner.

"Sometimes you have to do things you don't want to do," she says again.

WHO'S GOING TO KILL ME

It's a windy day, a rain storm blowing up from the south, everything clean and fresh. I'm at a corner, waiting to cross, when one of those cars with a metallic finish and dark windows, throbbing with rap, that you know is filled with little gangsta mothahfuckahs stops in the crosswalk just as the light turns. This broad, 35, 40, business type, professor maybe, lawyer, briefcase, power suit, goes up, kicks the door. Immediately the window comes down you see her yammering,
   "the music this"
   "the crosswalk that"
   "inconsideration of the other"
   Then she walks on, grinning, you can see she can hardly wait to tell her colleagues, lawyers, professors, whatevers, how she put these punks in their place.
   But of course what she doesn't see is these four little punks get out of the car taking their little
   .22's
   9 em em's
   .38's
out of their pants and my saying "Hey, man, let 'er go, she's my sister, she's crazy, she don't know what she's doin' half the time, hell all the time," praying they're looking for an excuse not to kill her, not to thread that phony ring-

letted yellow hair through her skull and knot it across her little self-satisfied mouth.

They say "Yeah, keep your crazy sister at home. Next time don't matter she's crazy."

But it's not over. A week later, a dirty yellow day, the sun like a lead weight pulling the sky down, I'm at a party, a little soiree, professional types except for me but I'm with my girlfriend, and there's this broad, she's telling these other professional types how she put these little assholes down, that's all they need, is to be shown their place, shown who's what.

I go over, say "Yeah, I heard about it."

She looks at me like who the fuck am I, she says, "How could you have heard about it, I only told a couple people?"

I say "Actually, I was there."

She looks at me.

I say "Actually, you almost got your dumb ass shot and if I or someone hadn't convinced those kids not to fuck you up you would be dead right now and this kind of fucking stupid-ass boasting I hear coming out of your mouth turns my stomach because I can just see someone—maybe me—getting his ass killed because of something you do, dig?"

There is quiet while everybody including my girlfriend stares at me like I got shit on my shoes, they just now figured out where the smell is coming from.

Then this broad says "No, really, where did you hear about it? Did so and so tell you?"

When I was in Iraq I knew that when I got killed it would be because some clerk in some office who never heard of me fucked up. Misfiled something, mistyped something. Something. And that's who this broad is. She's the clerk in the office in the city I've never been to who's going to kill me.

ON THE BUS

I used to work swing shift for the Census Bureau back when its regional office was a block from the Pike Place Market, and I took the bus to work from where I lived off of Aurora, north of Greenlake.

One afternoon I was seated by a window toward the rear of the bus. The bus was packed as it usually was at that time of day. Across the aisle two black teenagers were giving a white man a hard time, asking him how much money he had, demanding that he show them his wallet, and so on. The man appeared to be "developmentally disabled," by which I mean he was a little awkward in the way he moved—perhaps "uncoordinated" is a more accurate term—and he seemed slow mentally. Perhaps he had had a head injury. Perhaps the wiring defect in his brain was congenital.

Another man told the kids to leave the guy alone and they told him to mind his own business. Other people took notice—I could hear the buzz of talk like the distant whisper of a hive of bees—and the kids went to the front of the bus.

In a moment everybody, without a word, suddenly stood up. I did too, although I had no idea why. I had not thought to stand up, but I had risen at the same moment as everyone else. I think of the films of wildebeests running as a herd and then suddenly changing direction in unison. How do they communicate the intent to turn? How did we on the bus communicate the command, if it was a command—but no one of us was in charge of the others—to stand up?

I asked the man beside me what happened.

"They hit the bus driver." The bus driver was a short, wiry, middle-aged woman with red hair.

The bus had stopped and the front door was locked. The two kids ran from the front to the rear of the bus, but that door was locked too. One of them ran forward again. They were terrified—you could see the fear etched on their faces which appeared to have lost all their subcutaneous fat; the skin on them looked like parchment. Other people were starting to move about—small motions: the muscles working on a face, the opening and closing of a hand. Perhaps the release from tension. Perhaps only a kind of squirming.

Then the driver opened the front door and the kid at the front ran out. The kid in back pushed at the rear door, but the driver would not open it. The boy ran to the front and out the door that had remained open.

Only then did we, the other passengers, sit down.

The driver told us the police would be here soon and asked us not to leave the bus. We complied.

As I had seen nothing, I was permitted to leave a few minutes after the police arrived and I was able to get to my job on time. I was working then for an unforgiving boss.

But I wonder now if the bus driver believed she was saving those kids from a beating, or worse. I'm sure she did.

She seemed to be someone able to assess a situation quickly. And I wonder if I would have participated in the beating or murder of those kids. Before this happened, I would have said no, and I would have been certain of my answer. But I don't know why I stood up with the others, or, indeed, why any of us stood up. Might I do something else someday without knowing why I was doing it? I wonder if the others who were on that bus ask themselves why they stood up. I wonder if those two kids—they would be men now, if they are still alive—remember what happened that day on the bus coming from Seattle's north end, headed downtown.

A NIGHT AT THE IHOP

There used to be an International House of Pancakes on the corner of Brooklyn and Northeast Forty-third in the University District, just down from the Neptune theater. This was years ago. Decades. It was there and then it closed and then it was torn down in order to expand the parking lot that had served it.

One evening I took my son David there after a movie. We sat in a booth by a window looking out on the bare asphalt and mostly vacant stalls of the parking lot, and behind me, in the adjacent booth, were three kids. Not kids exactly—they were maybe nineteen or twenty years old—but a lot younger than me and only a few years older than David. As we ate our sandwiches I eavesdropped on the kids' conversation. David knew not to talk to me when I was eavesdropping and he silently concentrated on devouring his hamburger and then his fries. Oddly, he always ate his fries after finishing his sandwich.

It was apparent that the boy and one of the girls behind me were a couple and the other girl was a friend of theirs. There was some gossip about people who weren't there, all of whom the boy was sour on. It appeared that these three shared a house with some other people. This was common during the Seventies and early Eighties when money was tight, the divorce rate was climbing, and Seattle's population was growing again after the Boeing Bust of the early Seventies. Perhaps the boy was sour on their housemates because he and his girlfriend hadn't been together for very long and he wanted to sequester her from them.

After they gossiped, the boy and his girl began teasing each other about sex, about what she liked and what he wanted. All of the talk about sex was done through euphemism and allusion, as if by not speaking directly about it, they would prevent anyone listening to them—their friend; me, if they were aware that I was eavesdropping—from knowing what they meant. There was some shuffling around on the seat behind mine as they seemed to be feeling inside each other's clothing, or trying to. Perhaps only the boy was groping, because after thirty seconds or a minute, the girl said, "Don't do that," and the sounds of movement ceased. Then she said, "I have to use the bathroom," and then I saw a young blonde woman of average height or taller, with a pleasing figure, walk past me.

When she got up, she left what felt like a vacuum of silence, but this was filled in a moment by the other girl announcing, "I'm pregnant."

Immediately the boy said, "It's not mine."

"I don't think it's yours," the girl said.

There was silence again, but it didn't feel like a vacuum this time. Rather, there was a kind of energy that occupied it. The boy said, "It doesn't cost much to get rid of it nowadays."

"I know. I haven't decided what I'm going to do," the girl said.

"It can't be mine."

"I don't think it's yours. It probably isn't."

"It can't be. When do you think it happened?"

"Around the time we did it that time by the fireplace."

I heard the boy sigh. "It isn't mine," he said again.

"It probably isn't," the girl said. Then she said, "I don't know what I'm going to do."

That kind of energy-laden silence again. The girl said, "I should probably move out."

"I don't have any money," the boy said. "You don't have to move."

"No, I'm going to move out. I don't expect you to do anything. Maybe help me move. Carry boxes and things, I mean."

"Thank you," the boy said. "When do you think it will be?"

"The baby?"

"I meant the move."

"Oh. I haven't even looked for a place yet. I might move back with my sister."

"That's probably a good idea. If you need help. You might need help."

Neither of them had spoken with either cynicism or irony in their tone.

The boy's girlfriend came back from the restroom. She sat down and said something about something written on the wall in the stall. The boy said something but didn't laugh, and then he said, "Let's go."

He was very tall and rangy and had long hair a little darker than his girlfriend's. The other girl was shorter. She was thin and had mouse-colored hair.

After they left the restaurant I asked David if he had heard them. He had heard some of what they said, but hadn't been able to make sense of it.

"The boy and the blonde girl are boyfriend and girlfriend," I said.

"I got that," David.

"But the dark-haired girl is pregnant, and the baby may be his."

"Really?" David's eyes widened. He was shocked.

I nodded.

"What's going to happen?" He said it as though he were responding to a movie or a melodrama on TV.

I shrugged. "He already has a girlfriend."

"That's mean."

"Yes. For everyone."

"He should leave his girlfriend and marry the one that's pregnant and then he should make his first girlfriend pregnant and leave his other girlfriend, or his wife, and marry this girlfriend—the first one." David laughed. Then he said, "What's she going to do?"

"She doesn't know. She can get an abortion. That's what the boy wants her to do. Or she can have the baby. If she has the baby she can either keep it or give it away."

"Who would she give it to?"

"I don't know, but there are agencies that help with that sort of thing. They would try to find parents for it."

"Like orphanages?"

"Some are. Or the baby may go to foster parents until it's adopted."

While we were talking, a thin man with sharp features ran into the restaurant followed by another man who looked almost like him. Both men were in their twenties or early thirties. The second man had a short-bladed knife in his right hand and the man he was chasing ran around to the far side of the table nearest the entrance. David saw my eyes shift and he turned and together we watched the two men. Other than a waitress and two cooks, the only people in the restaurant besides us were a young man and woman in a booth on the other side of the dining room who were absorbed in conversation.

The man with the knife ran to his right around the table to try to get to the other man, but the other man ran just as far to his right around the table as the man with the knife ran. Then, as though by agreement, they reversed and ran to their left, keeping the same distance between them. All the while, both men were yelling angrily at each other in a language I didn't understand and the man with the knife was also crying.

Then the unarmed man broke out of the circular path he was following and ran over to the counter in front of the kitchen where there were coffee pots and a silverware tray and grabbed a steak knife out of the tray and returned to the table where his pursuer had stopped and was watching him. The newly armed man began to chase the man with the short-bladed knife to the right and then to the left until both men ran out of the restaurant, one after the other, still screaming. I couldn't see whether or not the one was crying still.

When they were gone, the waitress rushed to the door

and locked it. Then she started yelling about everybody being crazy and said she had had it, this was her last day, they could get someone else to do her job. She came over and asked if I wanted more coffee and said those two guys— Iranians or Arabs or something, she really couldn't tell the difference and honestly didn't care what they were—they came in last week and the same thing happened. It was over a woman, of course. Wasn't it always? The waitress, a young woman who had short, spiked hair, part of which was green, the rest a rich, chestnut brown, and who was about the age of the kids who had been sitting behind me, really didn't understand what it was about because she didn't speak their language, but they used to be friends, and they used to come in here a lot until the thing happened that made them enemies and one of them told her it had to do with the other guy's wife or sister or something, and a lot of it had to do with their culture, he said.

Just then we heard banging on one of the glass panes that made up the upper half of the door. It was one of the men with knives. The waitress yelled, "We're closed!" But the man continued to bang. "We're closed, goddamnit! Can't you understand American!"

Then she went to the door and unlocked it and it opened and the man with the steak knife ran inside with the man with the short-bladed knife after him. They ran back and forth around the table they had run around before until one of the cooks came out of the kitchen with a large skillet and yelled, "Put those goddamn knives down or I'll fuck you both up! That knife is mine! Put it down!"

Both men stopped running and stared at the cook who

raised the skillet as though to knock them on the head. The cook was not an especially large man but he clearly had meant what he said, and when he took a step toward them in addition to thrusting the skillet even farther into the air, the man with the steak knife quickly placed it on the table.

"This is my knife," the man with the short-bladed knife said in English.

"Then put it to fuck away," said the cook, and raised the skillet again after having lowered it. The man with the short-bladed knife folded it and put it in the front pocket of his pants.

"Now behave yourselves," the cook said, and returned to the kitchen.

The two men looked at each other and began to cry. Then they were in each other's arms, embracing and stepping back to touch each other's face or shoulder, then embracing again.

The couple from the far side of the dining room walked past the embracing men, gave money to the waitress who was manning the cash register now, and left. I read modest amusement on their faces.

David and I got up and went to the cash register. The two men were crying wholeheartedly and seemed to be saying things to each other that signified regret.

"I don't give a shit," the waitress said. "I'm still leaving. I took this shit job so I could support myself so I could go to school, but I haven't taken a class since I started working here."

"That was a kind of education," I said.

"A kind of education that won't get me a better job."

Walking to the car, I said, "Well, that was fun."

"Fun!" David said. "You liked that?"

"Sure. How often do you get to see something like that? And before that, we had the pregnant girl and her lover. Or ex-lover. What a fun evening! Didn't you think so?"

"I don't know. I didn't think of it like that."

"Well, you should."

"You're weird, Dad."

"*I'm* weird!"

I laughed, and David did too.

TRAGEDY IN THE DESERT

Some of the impulses and actions
we regret result from qualities we
have to possess in order to live.
—William Stafford

Once, returning to my car after a day of hunting jackrabbits just south of Perris, I stepped into a creosote bush. Although I had a personal rule not to step into a bush when in the desert, I was very tired and, rather than walk around it, I decided to walk through it. Immediately as I set my foot down, I felt a muscular movement under my boot. In an instant I was running, running until I was clear of that bush, clear of it, by fifty, a hundred feet. Stopped, I made certain my rifle was fully loaded. Then I went back to the bush where I saw, in the shade below the branches radiating out from their root into the hotter, drier air, a coiled rattlesnake, its tongue flicking, tasting the air for prey or enemies.

Enraged, I shot it and shot it and shot it until I had fired all of the seventeen rounds in my rifle's magazine. Then I reloaded and continued to shoot, until the snake's head hung beside its body by a single scaled shred of skin. Only then was I satisfied that I had killed it.

Years later, long after I had given up hunting, I acknowledged to myself my remorse at having killed that snake. Until then, that moment of rue, whenever I thought about it, I felt only the shards of fear and the rage I had experienced as I shot it again and again and again, reenacting the tragic condition of our species.

ALL AIR IS FINITE

I knew a boy who killed a man by dropping a rock off a bridge and through the windshield of his passing car. After two years the boy had convinced himself that the rock had dropped itself.

The hardest story I ever heard, though one that ever repeats itself, concerns a boy who, diving a shipwreck at ninety feet with his father, witnesses his father getting tangled in a murk of cables and cannot extricate him. Ultimately his father sends him to the surface—all air is finite, a son's no less than a father's—to locate help, but of course the only help he can find is the help that will bring up the body.

This is as far as the story goes.

But there are questions. What would the boy have told himself? Certainly he would recognize eventually that his father, grasping the fact of his imminent death, had saved his son by sending him off in search of illusory help. And inevitably the boy would have asked himself what more he could have done.

But would he have asked himself when exactly did he know his father would die? Was it when he left him? Was it during his ascent? Or was it only on that sun-bright surface, that more common world of foot motility and unencumbered speech, that he understood that all air is finite? Would the boy, after two years or three of grief, have persuaded himself to despise his father for dying as he committed his son to live?

What did the boy do with his life? Did he mutilate it with drugs? Did he end it with a gun? Did he hide in a monastery or a university? Did he marry, beat his wife, murder his children?

The boy who dropped the rock that dropped itself went to prison, served his time, got out. I lost track of him, though I heard stories, unverified.

The second boy got life.

R.I.P., LI'L HOMIE

Li'l Homie come up to me and say he want me to shoot
him. Sure, I say, where you want it? In the knee or the
arm? In the ear? In between those two big wolf teeth you
got in the front of your mouth? Where you want it? I'm
jokin' him, you see. Clownin' him. He say no, he want me
to kill him. He ain't jokin'. I see he ain't. I say, Li'l Homie,
I can't kill you, you my li'l homie. He shake his head, he
say, I need to die, I can't take this life no more. Li'l Homie,
I can't, I say. I love you, I can't kill you. He look at me then
for a long time, then he walk away.

He gets himself a rifle and he goes to Enemyland. To
the land of our enemies. That's only a couple blocks from
here. Four blocks. And he hists himself up on this store
building that's got this flat roof, and he plinks himself
some li'l children. Li'l enemy children. Five, six, seven
years old. Enemy children. And he come back to the club-
house and he say,

You know that dude on the t.v. who plink those li'l
kids? That me.

Other homies laughin' 'cause they don't believe him,
but I ain't laughin', 'cause I know he ain't lyin'. I see in
the way he says, he ain't lyin'. Plus there's the thing before,
when he asked me to shoot him.

Homie, I say, 'cause he ain't li'l no more. Homie, they

just kids. Li'l children. What they do to you?

They enemy, he say, size don't matter.

Size matter, I say.

We starin' at each other in the eyes now, neither of us backin' down. The others, they quiet, they not sayin' anything, they watchin' but they scared. They never seen Li'l Homie like this. You all go out of here, I say. And they go out.

You gonna wreck us, ain't you? I say.

Homie nods his head yeh.

Why you wanna do that? You spose to love your homies. He don't say nothin', but this big tear starts comin' out his eye at the corner by his nose. He don't wipe it away nor nothin'. Do you hate us? I say.

No, he say, almost as if they ain't no tear on his face.

Why you do this? I say. You know this gonna come back on us. How we explain killin' li'l kids?

Kill me, he say. And I say, That what this all about, ain't it?

He nod his head again yeh, but he don't say nothin'. He cryin' out both eyes now.

I can't kill you, homie. I love you even you don't love us no more, I say.

I'll do it again, he say. He cryin' in his voice now, he can't hide it no more. But I know he mean what he say. He'll do it no matter how much it hurt him or anybody.

Homie, I say, but I can't say no more 'cause I be cryin' too.

Please, he say.

Why, homie? Why?

I can't take livin' no more.

Why, homie? What be so hard on you? What make you special?

Nothin', he say. I'm just me.

He laugh then, and I think maybe it over, maybe he be Li'l Homie again. But then he take out this gun and he say, Send me out with love.

Homie...

And he put the front of the gun in his mouth and he pull that trigger before I could do a thing. And that how he went out. And I wish to God I done what he asked me, 'cause he went out alone and I could have sent him with love.

Li'l Homie. R.I.P.

THE LONELY DIVER

Harry went into the water a mile east of Alki Beach. Twenty years earlier there had been an abandoned cannery here, its windows broken, the green paint on its sides worn past flaking and slowly disappearing under stress of rain and sun. Divers called it the ugliest building in Seattle and used it as a point of reference, as in: "Go out toward Alki. Look for the ugliest building in Seattle. I'll meet you just to the left of it and we'll go in there."

Now, instead of the cannery, there was a park. Grass, sun shelter, rest rooms. Visually an improvement, but it brought people. Harry did not like to be around people he did not know well. He would look at them and guess what they were capable of, but he didn't know what they would do, or when. He was a rehabilitation counselor in a prison for children.

Today he was diving without a partner. When he dived alone he liked to go to a place he knew, where he was familiar with the currents and was not likely to run into discarded fishing line. Fifteen years ago, maybe more, he had gotten tangled in line near the Fauntleroy ferry dock while swimming through a kelp bed and had to rely on his partner to cut him out of it. He had been snagged before he knew it. Still, if there were no fish to attract fishermen, there was little to attract him. Fauntleroy was not a place he would dive alone now. In any event, there was only a vestige of the kelp bed that had been there. Most of it had been torn away by a gale a few years back.

The day had started out clear but by the time he got in the water a thin layer of cloud concealed not only the sun but the entire sky, so that what he could see beneath the surface was negligible. There was a small school of striped perch and he had a glimpse of a dogfish in the murk at the edge of visibility. He was out of the water after thirty minutes, though he had air enough for another fifteen.

He went out again a few days later, this time to the pilings at Edmonds. He was with Bruce. The pilings were what remained after Chevron took out the oil pipeline and dismantled the dock where the tankers used to put in. Though it was the beginning of winter, there had been several warm, sunny days and the algae bloom was so thick they could hardly see their hands until they got down to thirty feet. At the bottom they saw a large cabezon, some tube worms attached to the pilings, and a sponge that Bruce picked up and used in the pretense of washing his armpits. He often played the clown and his silliness as often made Harry laugh.

When they came out of the water Harry found that the fin strap behind his left ankle had been cut through so that only a narrow strip of rubber held it together. When he looked closely he saw serrations, tooth marks, at the edges of the cut. He remembered then that as he had settled himself on his belly to observe the cabezon, he had pushed his foot back and something had hit him. He had thought a piece of trash had fallen on him, maybe a bit of rotting timber. It didn't hurt so he didn't think more of it, but now he thought it must have been a wolf eel. He had seen one here before, in ten feet of water, eating a rock crab.

The next week they went to the same place. It had gotten cold again and Bruce wanted to see what he could see with good visibility. Harry had a bad feeling even before they went in the water and he was tired in a way he couldn't explain. His sense that something was wrong intensified and halfway to the end of the pilings, while they were still on the surface, he told Bruce he wanted to turn back.

There was a lot of chop accompanied by tidal swells and they decided to submerge and swim back to the beach under water. When Harry took his first breath his regulator went into free-flow. He couldn't stop it; air was gushing through his mouthpiece too fast to breathe it in. He went to the surface, Bruce following, and inflated his buoyancy compensator and asked Bruce to turn off his air. They snorkeled back to the beach.

Harry had his tank refilled at the dive shop beside the small marina a quarter mile from the pilings and rented a regulator there. They had decided to do a night dive in the underwater park north of the ferry terminal. They were into winter now and they had only an hour to wait until the gray northern light was gone. They sat over coffee at the Skipper's near the terminal.

Bruce had recently separated from a woman he had lived with for years. Harry had always enjoyed diving with him and Bruce was eager to get into it again. Janice had convinced him to give it up, he said, after they started talking about getting married. It wasn't the risk, he thought, because he had taken up mountaineering after he stopped diving and she hadn't said anything about that.

Harry knew Janice and it did not make sense to him that she had insisted Bruce quit diving; the three of them used to dive together. But it was true she hadn't gone out in a while when he gave it up. Maybe there had been an agreement: he gives up something, she gives up something. Each sacrifices something for the marriage. Harry had known other couples to do this. In any case, he liked Bruce and was glad to be diving with him again.

Setting his cup down, Bruce said he thought he and Janice had made a mistake by getting engaged when they were just fine living together. He hoped they would remain close, or become close again after her anger had lost some of its bite.

"She's hurt," Harry said.

"Well, yeah." Bruce laughed ruefully. "She's kind of unpleasant to be around right now."

"Are you still seeing each other?"

"We're trying to. It's not like it was, but maybe it will be."

Harry didn't say anything.

"She'll never forgive me." He gave that laugh again.

Harry didn't say anything.

"I wish I hadn't asked her to marry me. I wish I hadn't broken off the engagement." A grim smile. No laugh.

"Do you still want to marry her?"

"I never did. I mean if I wanted to get married, I'd want to marry her. But I don't want to get married. Not now, anyway. Maybe not ever. I'll be like you."

"I was married once."

"Yeah? I didn't know that." Bruce looked at him. "What else don't I know about you? Are you keeping secrets?"

Harry laughed.

"How's the work?" Bruce asked.

Harry shrugged. He said, "We had a suicide. Not my unit, one of the girls' cottages. Hanged herself in the shower. I didn't know her, fortunately."

"Jesus," Bruce said. "What do you do in a situation like that?"

"I wasn't there. I was in my own cottage when it happened. We locked down. All the cottages locked down while Security dealt with it. Oh, you mean personally?" Harry thought for a moment. "I don't know. I don't know what I do. I try to help the kids deal with it. There are always some who feel responsible, even if they didn't know her. As if there was something they could have done to prevent it."

"There've been others?"

"This is the third since I started there. There have been dozens of attempts. It's a pretty unhappy place."

"I don't know how you do it."

Harry pushed back from the table. "Ready to get wet?"

"I owe you an explanation," Harry said. They were in the car. "About why I wanted to turn back."

"At the pilings? You had a premonition, didn't you?"

"How did you know that?"

"It was pretty obvious. You said you wanted to abort and then your regulator fell apart. It doesn't take a genius to put that together. Plus, you've had them before, haven't you? Didn't you used to get them when you were parachuting?"

"Once, yeah. I forgot I told you about that."

"And you were right again. I trust you, old man. We've always had that agreement, remember? If one of us doesn't feel good about it, we abort the dive. Right?"

"Right."

"Okay then. How do you feel about this one?"

"It's going to be something to behold."

"My feeling exactly."

They were in the parking lot and Harry pulled into a space. Two other cars were in the lot but no one was on the beach except for an elderly woman walking a terrier. They changed into their wet suits in the rest room at the far end of the park. It was cold and their suits were still wet from the afternoon. Both of them were shivering. By the time Harry got his tank on he wanted only to get in the water and get moving.

The visibility was good and they submerged about twenty minutes from the beach. He could see Bruce eight or ten feet ahead, swimming toward the wreck. There were two wrecks actually, and they passed the remains of the first, about the size of a dory, and went for the one nearer the ferry dock. They were sailing along the bottom— that was how it felt, as though he were sailing with the wind behind him, so effortless was the swim in the cold, almost still water—and found the boat at forty feet. Bruce gestured and they went up over the top of it and started down toward its deck.

To Harry's right, out of the gloom, a small lingcod swam into the beam of his lamp, turned and swam back into the dark. As he approached the deck, the fish came again, mouth agape, teeth screening the pit, and again was gone. It was young, twelve or fifteen pounds. Harry pressed air into his buoyancy compensator and hung in the water, motionless, waiting for it to come a third time. When it did, he saw a gray film where its right eye should have been, and that it always swam away to its left, following its good eye.

He trailed his light after it, saw its shadow run along the ruined boat deck, saw it turn again toward the light, now fully in the beam, now gone. Bruce was resting on his knees on the deck. As the fish passed, its blind eye to him, he put his hand out, then pulled it back before the fish ran into it.

How had it happened? Had it been hooked, then the hook torn out? Had it been attacked? What would have attacked it? Whatever happened, it must have happened here. It could not have found its way here half-blind. It would never find its way anywhere else now. Circle after circle, it would swim until it was no longer able to. What was it Harry saw in its good eye? Madness? Rage? Did it know it followed only itself? Be careful, Harry told himself. What are you giving it and what is there without you? He hung in the water, his lamp in his hand. The fish followed itself into light, into darkness, into light…

Harry checked his air. He had seven hundred pounds left. How long had he been hanging here? He kicked down to where Bruce was and showed him an open hand and two fingers from the other one. Bruce checked his gauge, then showed it to him. He had a little less than Harry. Bruce jabbed his thumb toward the surface and they ascended.

Harry took his regulator out of his mouth. "Wow."

"Right." Bruce looked around as though to get his bearings. "Look." Perched on a resting raft less than five meters away, a cormorant was staring at them. It took off, almost belly flopping into the water before it caught air. It was about the size of a herring gull and a half again.

As they were changing into their clothes, Harry said, "I wish we could have killed it. It's going to starve."

"It's a state park. You can't do anything about what you see. If the rangers catch you, they'll fine the shit out of you."

"You can't do anything about what you see."

"That's what I said."

"I know."

"In a way, that's what I like most about diving. You're the alien. It's like you're a guest on another planet and one of the rules is you can look, but you can't touch, at least not in a protected area."

"Even if you see suffering."

"Yeah. Even then. It's rough."

"Well, you're right when you say it's like being on another planet. For me, it's like stepping into a science fiction novel, and the beings in it don't give a damn about you as long as you don't try to eat them. It's their world and you're going to be there for only a few minutes. The problem comes when we care about them. We want to put an end to their suffering, or what we imagine is their suffering, even if we have to kill them to do it."

"Whoa, Harry. You've been reading too much. I just do it for fun."

"Oh no, my furry friend. I know you. You're lying to yourself."

"I know, but it's a good lie." Bruce giggled like a ten-year-old. "My furry friend," he said, looking at Harry. He repeated the child's laugh.

Harry had used to dive with a man who had retired from teaching. Harry asked him once if he missed it. Every day, he said. He missed the kids. He missed watching them develop into something more than they had been, or at least something different. But he did not miss the administration. He did not miss its insistence on teachers giving up something that worked for something that didn't. He did not miss taking orders from people who had no experience of the classroom, or who ignored what they had learned when they were teachers. He did not miss the ideologues, the religionists, or the false patriots. Eventually he realized that his daily experience with kids no longer compensated for everything about the administration that so weighed on him. He felt his life no longer had balance and he decided to retire. He became a fine printer, using an old Chandler and Price letterpress to produce chapbooks and the occasional perfect-bound book.

Harry thought about what Mark had said, especially the part about compensation and balance, and thought too about what he might do if he gave up the prison. His father had left him some money when he died a couple of years ago and Harry speculated he could live off it for a while if he had to. He wrote a letter of resignation, leaving space for date and signature, folded it into a small rectangle and put it in his wallet.

They were Dungeness. Harry was at seventy feet when he saw them, Bruce on his right and a little above. The crab were moving in a column of twos toward the beach, coming up from where it was too dark to see them and too deep to dive. Every few meters Harry saw one or two out at either side of the column, like flank scouts. Two crab in the column marching side by side, grasped something thin and white, like a piece of a tee shirt, between them, the left claw of one and the right claw of the other clamped on its far edges. Only these two carried anything; the others followed them at regular intervals or marched ahead of them. Harry swam to the front of the column where it was nearing a savannah of eelgrass. Ten meters ahead of the main body was a cluster of five proceeding forward in a star configuration, and to each side of the star, ten or twelve feet out, was a single crab moving in unison with those that made up the star's points.

Harry motioned to Bruce to come toward him. They were above the foremost part of the column, the forward scouts in the eelgrass now. Bruce descended until he was a meter above the column. It stopped, the crab directly below him standing erect, their claws up. Bruce pushed at the water before him with his hands, and kicked. He began to rise.

Harry went out toward the point element and swam down, intending to grab one of them. They scattered and he selected the one closest to him and went after it into the eelgrass. It was surprisingly fast, faster than he was. He had chased crab before, for fun or food, but he had never come on one that could outrun him. He was astounded at its speed. He wanted to try another, but Bruce was in front of him, showing him with his hands that he had only six hundred pounds of air left. Harry looked at his gauge. The needle was a little below five hundred. Harry nodded his head and they swam together toward the beach.

"Have you ever seen anything like that before?"

"No. Have you?"

Harry shook his head. "I've heard of lobster migrations, but I've never heard of crab doing it."

"That one little guy was fast. I saw you running after him."

"Yeah. I wonder if they're faster just after they molt and have new shells."

They were on the beach at Mukilteo, stripped down to their bathing suits, letting the sun warm them. The drying

salt pulled the skin tight on Harry's back and face. It was
a wonderful sunny day. When they went in the water, it
had been gray and drizzly. Harry felt very good. He felt
a sense of completeness as he hardly ever did after a dive,
and never in anything else he did. It was the combination
of sun and warmth and the salt drying and the effort he
had made in going after that crab.

"What do you think of that white thing those two crab
were holding onto?"

"That thing like a shirt, or what was left of one? Yeah.
I'm trying not to think about that," Bruce said.

"The things we've seen," Harry said. "Remember that
half-blind lingcod at Edmonds?"

"Yeah. Yeah."

"And that skate as big as a barn door?"

"You told me about it. They don't get as big as barn
doors, though."

"Little barns. For Shetland ponies."

Bruce gave out a laugh that ended in a snort.

"I once saw two eels mating," Harry said. "They were
pure white. I mean whiter than anything I'd ever seen, or
seen since. At first I didn't know what I was looking at.
All I saw was this white ball about the size of a soccer ball,
about twenty feet down. This was in Samoa at a break in
the reef by Faga'alu."

"Say that again."

"Faga'alu. It's the name of a village. I lived there for
a while after I left the army. After a lot of things. I was
snorkeling and I saw this white ball on the sand right
below me. And then it split apart and it was two snow-

white eels, whiter even than snow. And they faced each other and then came together again, almost in a fury, it happened so fast and so violently. Maybe it was real fury, whatever that might be to eels. In a second they were so wrapped around each other you could not see where one left off and the other began. I remember thinking, 'Maybe that's why they call it balling.' But how many people have seen eels balling? I had a friend there, Chuck Brugman, who had spent most of his life diving in the Pacific, and I asked him if he'd ever heard of white eels, but he hadn't."

"Maybe they were congers."

"Congers are gray."

"Albino congers?" He was being impish.

"Who knows. Though this was in daylight and the sun was directly on them."

"Yeah, you'd think they'd stay indoors during the day and watch TV. Or sleep. They could have been vampire albino congers."

Harry stared at him. Bruce laughed but Harry continued to stare.

"Don't say it," Bruce said. "You're thinking, 'Speaking of balling, what's Janice been up to?' But I don't want to hear it."

Harry laughed. He couldn't help it. "Goddamn! We've known each other too long."

Bruce laughed again, not the little-boy laugh or the snorting laugh or any other that bespoke something else, but one that was straightforward and unaffected, and then he said, "I didn't know you lived in Samoa. My grandfather was there during the war. World War Two."

"I had an odd experience in Samoa once. I was diving with Chuck on the reef at Faganeanea—"

"Jeez. These names. Call it something else. Call it Albert."

"You call it Albert." Harry was annoyed. He wanted to tell this story and he wanted to tell it without bowdlerizing it. "So I was out with Chuck and we left the boat and were following the anchor chain down, and Chuck peeled off at about forty feet—he had said he was going to look for a particular shell he had spotted there on another dive— but I decided to go a little farther and then, without even thinking about it, I was on the bottom at a hundred and thirty-five feet."

"Were you using nitrogen?"

"They don't have that there. Just compressed air."

"Jesus, Harry."

"I know. But that's what I did. I had expected to feel the effects of narcosis—you know, nausea, loss of peripheral vision—"

"I don't get nauseated."

"Okay, but I do. But this time I didn't. So I'm on the bottom and I look around and in the distance is a blue light, like a wall coming up off the floor of the ocean, like the aurora borealis but a bright, metallic blue, and I start swimming toward it—"

"Jesus."

"I know. And I swim for a while but I'm not getting any closer, and then it occurs to me: I'm alone at a hundred and thirty-five feet and I'm swimming toward something that may not exist and I'm gobbling air like there will always be more than I need, and I check my air gauge and there's enough left so that, if I suck every last ounce out of the tank, I can get back to the surface even with decompression. And so I go back to the anchor chain and start climbing back up. I pass Chuck on the way—he's still messing around on the reef, near the surface now—and I wave to him but I don't stop. It's really hard to get air now. It's like I'm looking for it, but it's at a premium and it's hiding—well, you know how it feels to run out of air. And I pop the surface and clamber up on the boat and take my gear off and wait to see if I get a headache. Sometimes, if I haven't decompressed long enough, I get a headache, but this time I don't. And then Chuck is on the surface and he hands me his fins and he gets himself up onto the boat and he asks me if I saw that big blacktip on the reef, he was trying to point it out to me when I was on my way up, but either I didn't see him sign or I didn't understand what he was saying. Which was probably to my benefit because I couldn't have stopped, shark or no shark."

"That's why you should always leave some air in your tank. You don't know what's going to happen on your way in. Or up."

"I know. I'm real careful now. Honest. I do wonder about that blue light though, what it was, or was it only in my head. And was there something on the other side of it, or is that how everything ends."

"Jeez, Harry, cut it out. You're making me nervous. How come you didn't have a premonition about all of this before the dive? Or did you?"

"No."

"Well, where are they when you really need one?"

"I sometimes ask myself that."

"Did you tell Chuck about the blue light?"

"No. I didn't want him to think I was a fool."

"I don't know who's the fool, to separate like that. Both of you were diving alone."

"Well, I used to think that as far as Chuck was concerned, if you were in the ocean at the same time he was, you were buddies."

"Is that when you started to like diving solo?"

"I don't know. I never thought about it. I don't know."

At fifteen feet, he saw a brown rockfish nestled against a black rock. Some of its color was so light as to appear yellow. It was odd that it was so still. As he swam nearer, it barely moved, perhaps an inch or two, and then it settled back against the rock. Had the rock not been there, the fish would have gone completely onto its side. Its mouth opened and closed as if it were gasping for breath, though of course it was not. But its gills were working, so he knew it was alive, if in trouble.

He swam farther out. The water was unusually clear. He had never seen such luxuriant floral growth in the Sound. A plant whose name he could never remember but which reminded him of a juniper tree extended twenty feet toward the surface. He saw flounder and some blue perch and a couple of neon green gunnels. There were plenty of jellyfish feeding on those white anemones with the fluffy crowns. He almost swam into one with five-foot-long tentacles. It was the largest he'd seen outside of the tropics or California. He could see bits of white fluff through its skin.

On the way back to the beach, he found the rockfish in the same place he had seen it earlier. He touched its head with his finger, but it didn't move. Neither its mouth nor its gills moved. A slight tidal surge raised him off the bottom and he took advantage of it to coast in to shore.

All morning his shirt hung wrong on him, the neck sliding to one side, sliding again after he adjusted it. And all morning his tee shirt under it lay like needles on his skin, his body vaguely in pain. It was as though walking, sitting, standing, he were askew, as though he were somehow out of alignment. Getting into his wet suit, his muscles ached with an intensity beyond aching, and the skin on his arms and torso burned as though aflame, though only in patches. Yet he did not think to stop. Rather, it was as if he were bound to do what he would, regardless of his fear.

They were diving off Columbia Beach. The water was calm, there was no wind. The bottom was sand and silt held by eelgrass. They were near the ferry dock; it would be difficult to get confused about direction even if you didn't have a compass.

They were in only twelve feet of water when he lost Bruce. Bruce was on his right and then he wasn't. He wasn't anywhere. Harry came to the surface and waited. Then he snorkeled back to the beach. A boy ten or eleven was walking toward him on the path from the restaurant parking lot above the rocks overlooking the beach. A man was behind the boy about forty feet. Harry asked the boy if he'd seen another diver within the last few minutes. The boy shook his head. Harry took his weight belt off, then his tank and buoyancy compensator. The boy and the man were watching the water that was so motionless now it might have been freighted with oil. The sun's glare off the surface forced Harry to turn his eyes away. He had the sensation that he had stepped outside of time and he looked at his watch to see how much time had passed since they entered the water. He asked the man to call the Coast Guard and the Sheriff's Office. He would wait where he was in case Bruce turned up.

The man had just started up the hill when Bruce stood up out of the water. He had a rockfish thrashing on the shaft of his spear and he was carrying his fins. His lips moved and then he let go of the spear and fell into the water.

"I can't breathe. I don't know what's wrong."

Harry got Bruce's weights and tank and buoyancy compensator off and, with the help of the man, got him to the beach and laid him on his back on the sand.

"I can't breathe."

He hardly had the words out when his irises rolled up inside his head. Harry performed CPR, alone at first, then with another man who suddenly appeared until the ambulance arrived and the medical technicians took over. When Harry compressed his chest, Bruce's eyes rolled forward, then rolled back when Harry stopped to blow into his mouth. But after a few minutes they froze halfway up under the lids. By the time the ambulance got there, Bruce's lips were turning blue.

The mound of earth beside the grave was dry. It must have been excavated yesterday, maybe even the day before, Harry thought. Then he thought, Of course it was dug yesterday. Who's going to come out here at dawn to dig a grave?

He had not seen Janice in almost two years. He had forgotten how compact she was, how boyish her face. He had always expected to see a smudge of dirt on her cheek or nose. He saw Bruce's father whom he had met once, but did not say anything to him. Bruce's father saw him too, but also chose not to speak.

Walking to his car after the service, he heard a woman's heels and turned and saw Janice walking rapidly in his direction.

"Harry."

The embrace felt good. Her fragrance was nice.

"I hoped I would see you."

"It's good to see you," he said.

"His family ignored me. Even Jessica. It was as if we had never met."

"They always were sort of self-contained. They ignored me too."

"It was his heart, wasn't it? Somebody said it was."

"That's what it looked like. I don't know if they did an autopsy."

"His uncle also died of a heart attack when he was

really young. His father must be wondering about the genes he passed on."

"Does his father think like that?"

"I don't know. I didn't know him very well. You were there, weren't you? With Bruce? When he died?"

"Yes."

"I'm sorry."

Harry nodded his head.

"He was a good friend to me," Janice said. "He was my good friend." Harry thought she would cry after she said it the second time, but all there was was a catch in her throat which she quickly swallowed. "Even after all this time. I could tell him anything, because he knew me so well."

She was looking at the pavement. She was smiling. She looked up at him.

"You haven't changed, Harry. I was hoping you hadn't. It's nice when something remains the same."

They were standing at his car. The morning chill had faded and the sun was warm on his face.

"What about you? How have you been?" he asked.

"I've been well. I'm in the doctoral program now."

"Arizona?"

"Yes. Archeology. I actually like it. I was surprised that I took to it so well. I was afraid I would hate it."

Was her front tooth chipped? No, that was his imagination.

"Well," he said.

"I have to go. I have to catch a plane at one. I have to be at a conference in the morning and I still need to rehearse

my presentation. It's okay, I rented a car. Did I tell you I
met someone? I'll call you and tell you about him."

One of the kids told Harry that Brien had broken his
window. Mike went to check on him while Harry opened
the blood-spill kit, put on gloves, gown, boots, started for
Brien's room. Halfway there, Mike met him, said blood
was everywhere. Harry stopped his progress, asked Mike to
fasten the gown's ties behind him, it was flapping between
his legs. (Time, time—everything takes forever. But this
was the age of AIDS, and the boy had been a prostitute.)
     Brien was sitting on his bed, his back against the far
wall. His left arm was extended—there were fresh cuts but
they had stopped bleeding. His right hand was pressed
against the side of his neck. Harry thought he may have
cut his neck or stabbed himself and was trying now to
stanch the flow of blood. There was blood on his right hand
but it had dried—it must have come from his punching
the window. The right side of his head and torso were
in shadow. Maybe two seconds had passed since Harry
opened the door to his room. Harry was standing at its
threshold. He asked Brien what was wrong, then stepped
into the room.
     Brien had a large shard of glass in his right hand and
was holding it against his neck. When Harry saw it he
drew back. He said, "Come on, Brien. Give it to me."
Brien was terribly frightened. He was nearly unconscious
with fright. Suns burned dimly in his pale eyes. Harry felt
his balance shift. In Brien's gray eyes Harry saw worlds he

did not know.

Brien made a quick downward motion with his hand and Harry heard something tear. Before Harry could move, Brien replaced the glass against his neck. Harry saw no fresh blood. Then—he didn't know why; he could think of nothing else to do—he grasped Brien's other hand and pressed it gently. As though he had been waiting for this specific signal, Brien threw the glass down on his bed and Mike came in and picked it up. Harry looked at Brien's neck where he had stroked the glass across it. It was raw but was not bleeding.

For a moment after Mike took Brien out of his room Harry sat on his bed, pulling himself out of Brien's eyes, away from the planets orbiting his fear. For a moment, two...

Until he reached sixty feet he had not known what he intended, but at sixty feet he decided to continue down into the pit where, decades earlier, they had dredged the bottom to allow the oil tankers in. Ninety feet and down. In a moment he would feel a rush of heat roll up his body, beginning at his feet and washing like a wave to his head, always, for him, the first indication of nitrogen narcosis. Then he would lose his peripheral vision and get the taste of bile in his mouth. At a hundred and twenty feet his skin would get numb, as though it were covered with an additional layer immune to tactile sensation, and his mind would split from itself. Part of it would observe everything around him and another part would tell him that the first part was lying and that he should not believe what it saw and heard. Once, only once, did a third part reveal itself, and it told him that he should not believe either the first part of his mind or the second part, neither what he saw and heard nor the doubting of them.

But he did not experience either the doubt or the doubt of both doubt and certainty this time. At a hundred and thirty-five feet he leveled off and aimed for a wall of sapphire light in the distance. His body was very warm and he was sweating inside his wet suit. He swam for several minutes but he seemed to get no closer and he began to question how this shimmering blue glow could exist in a place without sun, where light graduated in its quality only from dusk to deep night. He began to wonder if he had made a mistake by going so far and he began to ascend.

MONDAY MORNING IN EARLY SEPTEMBER

Everything was pink that day; even God's own sky looked pink to me, except for the red of that girl's hood. When I saw her I thought immediately how sad she looked, even though I couldn't see her face. Now, of course, I understand that it was my own sadness I saw on her.

She was sitting against the wire fence that surrounds the school where I was taking my granddaughter to enroll her. Her arms opened out away from her body and her palms were up so that I almost expected to see stigmata. Both girls, my granddaughter and the dead girl, were dressed in pink. The dead girl was wearing a pink sweat suit, pants and shirt, a designer suit really, not made for running or gymnastics. Her feet were naked. If she had been wearing shoes, one of the neighborhood children wore them now. A paper bag was over her head. It was not pink but a deep reddish-brown. When I got closer I saw that it was not paper but a cloth handbag, one you could buy in a store that imports from Mexico or South America. Before it became reddish-brown it had been a cottony white. Maybe it was this girl's. Maybe she had been shot by another girl who had put her own bag over this girl's head. But probably not. Not that another girl might not have shot her, but she wouldn't have ruined her own handbag. As I was reaching to pull it off, I suddenly felt overwhelmingly tired, but I wanted to close her eyes. I knew they would be open.

When I touched the bag it was hard and stiff, so I knew she had been dead for a while. When my granddaughter saw the girl's face, she screamed and brought her small hands to her own face. I had forgotten she was with me. I told her to go back to the car and I watched her as she ran across the street, her pink skirt bouncing up off her little bottom. I felt so tired I could hardly bear it. And so I drew down the eyelids on that poor, destroyed face, as you would close the blinds in your living room against the bright sun, and they stayed closed, though I was afraid they wouldn't.

Once when my son was in the war, he and his friends, the other soldiers he was with, were ambushed. His best friend—another boy from the neighborhood, but who Junior knew only casually back home—got killed in the ambush. They had been through so much bad together and now he had got killed. And after he died, immediately after, and maybe some others had died too, Junior and the other soldiers who remained sat down to eat while they waited for the helicopter to come. And as Junior ate his lunch, his best friend watched him with his dead eyes. And my son said to me a year later, or maybe two, that he hadn't felt a thing but tired as he ate his lunch. Not then, anyway. I do believe, I am absolutely certain, that my son took his own life because he couldn't forgive himself for not closing his friend's eyes, for not allowing him his earned peace.

Maybe that is why it was so important to me to close

this poor girl's eyes, so that no other child would have to see them, although it was not clear to me then why I needed to do this. But I wish I had been alone. I wish my granddaughter had not been with me. I wish this poor girl who could not have been fifteen years old had not died, nor my son, nor any other mother's son or daughter.

JEROME GOLD is the author of sixteen books, including *In the Spider's Web* and *Paranoia & Heartbreak: Fifteen Years in a Juvenile Facility*, memoirs based on the years he spent as a juvenile rehabilitation counselor in a prison for children, and *Sergeant Dickinson* and *The Moral Life of Soldiers*, fictions based in part on his experience in the Vietnam War. He lives near Seattle, Washington.